ISBN-13: 978-1-948920-16-2
ISBN-10: 1-948920-16-6
for more books, visit Pski's Porch:
www.pskisporch.com

Printed in U.S.A.

Transversal

by Fin Sorrel

This one goes out to the Natty Daddy Zombie club.
Fun times, Y'all.

Author's note: Feel free to select chapters, and read them at random. I stuck to my poem as the bone structure, where I dumped on meat and cheese, and salad and made a sandwich of a story, so don't fret, it's just gonna be weird, and can be read out of order. In fact it is encouraged, by me, its author.

This book is for Frosty the snowman, who is a very special man! And, goes out to those in the resistance who spend their lives teaching.

This book belongs to the akashic tree of records.

(In larva) appeared in Fur lined ghettos #9 (salo press)

Danio appeared in 5th wall

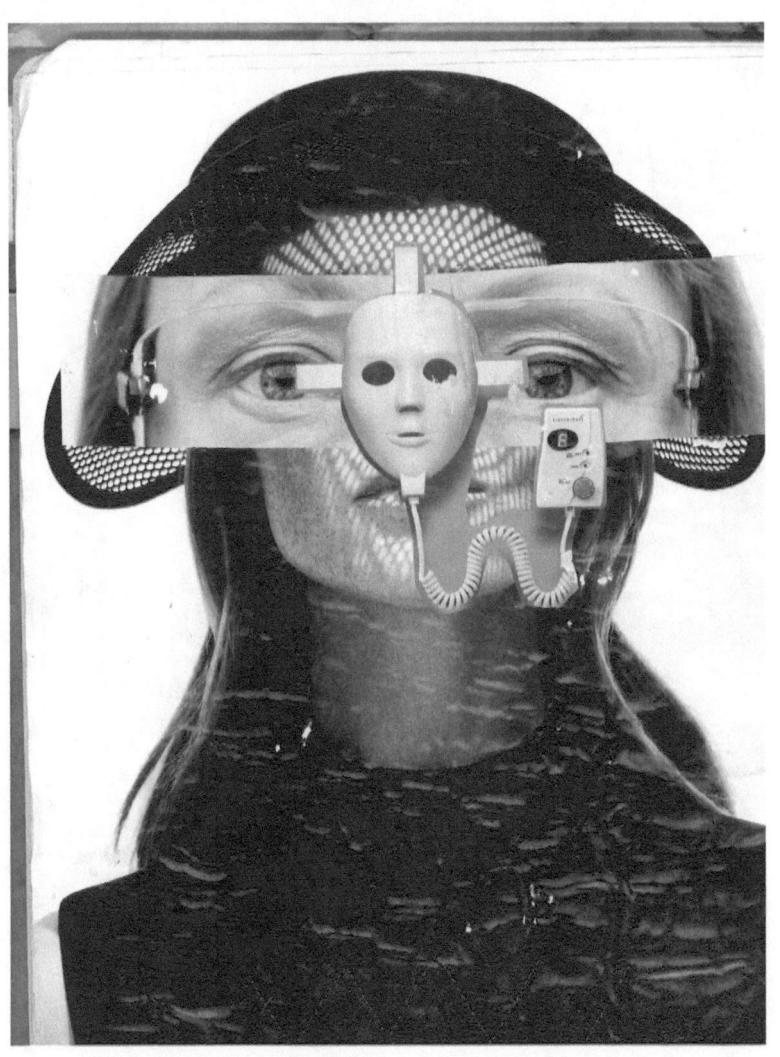

BOOK ONE: A RANT ON THE NEXT SIMULATIONS

"He who fights with monsters should be careful lest he thereby become a monster. And if thou gaze long into an abyss, the abyss will also gaze into thee."

- Friedrich Nietzsche, *Beyond Good and Evil*

"America is not so much a nightmare as a non-dream. The American non-dream is precisely a move to wipe the dream out of existence. The dream is a spontaneous happening and therefore dangerous to a control system set up by the non-dreamers." -William S. Burroughs

"Look at your hands."

I sit up on the floor in the back of a large italian theater, staring at the white gloves as they blur together into the center of my vision. People are about to watch a movie. I am in the last row of seats behind them. The room is packed with people eating popcorn, and sipping drinks. I take off my kid gloves, and toss them into the air above me, where they disappear, taken in by a vacuum sucking slurp sound. I snap my fingers, and come to; see the exit sign, see the velvet curtain, its folds and ruffled waves.

The lights are low, a red hue. I'm resting my head on my sweatshirt, I've been sleeping here. The coughing is what has woken me up. I grumble, toss my sweatshirt. My throat's fucked up from cigarettes. Incessantly hacking, the fluids in my nose and throat press forward, exposing tissues. This is not good, I need to get some water, now.

I quickly rummage through my side bag, and go blank, (back slash, dot.) blank, white sheets of drawing paper, napkins, scarves, a pillow case, cozy stuffing, no water. Ugh, crumble. Paper, what do I need this for? "Okay I'll get up." I mutter. My hands are delicate shivering things, like pale white sheets, they blow through the bag, investigating its contents again, and find matches, a wallet full of money, but nothing drinkable. Maybe concessions will have water. My fingers take a turn, searching deep in the side bag, I climb in and root around, stretching the cloth, my body insistent, fluid, clogged, exploring, and snaky. I'm dribbling the contents, all gold, I'll need it later, but where is my bottle for water? I am happy I have a Halloween mask, but what good is this for thirst. I throw it down, the masque twirls up to animate into a newborn fawn, wobbles by on its newfound legs, and I swoon at her briefly,

"Ahh, you're cute." I say. My eyes are open wide, but I spooked her, my voice was too loud, and she tramples off, outta the bag, through the theater, where she disappears.

"Legs, I have legs, and I like my legs like I like my spaghetti, when you throw it at the ceiling it sticks!" Standing up for the first time, I make way down the hallway, through the bag, whistling a tune. I need to stay wild, and limber here, or the others will … do something … nasty .. or uncalled for … and I refuse to fight, because everytime I do, I feel like I'm swinging under water, and my arms won't throw a punch fast, heavy with the weight, so I just stopped fighting long ago. There's no point.

Nineteen thirty two Paris jazz.

A drop of knowledge: Quitting alcohol can be deadly, many die every day in the united states. Drop of knowledge:

"… in Folk magic and Hoodoo etc. the use of bones (especially in Voodoo) are important, as well as chickens for their feathers, feet and eggs. So now we are looking at some unusual stuff here." (1)

Two familiar voices in the back row are talking, and their words come toward me.

"I know those people. It's my dad and my mom." Or is it my grandma? I can't make her out. But I know it's my dad with someone.

"The chicken's foot works by magically "scratching" one's would-be thief with its nails. It is a warning to those who would want to do you wrong. It is a warning symbol to the would-be

8

thief that if you steal my shit, I am going to hurt you in a way you have never known.

This is similar to seeing a skull and crossbones on a bottle of liquid, which tells you that if you drink this liquid, you are going to die or become very ill." (2) The other voice says, munching down popcorn.

"Yeah, I mean it's one experience to see the world, to just waste a world, is a delicate matter,"

"I know it, machines, drugs?" He starts counting on his fingers. "the funny bastards they are?"

"Oh yeah, definitely.Water helps Purify the body flushing out Toxins that keep us more susceptible to Mind Control from the Government & keeps us enslaved to the material world." (4)

"And cigarette butts. If you want to paint with them you can use those as paint brushes, but a dream about a japanese painter... From ... munch munch, Popcorn's good huh? From Japan ... I hear." I hear this. They are talking about me. The homeless man in the back of their theater. Maybe it's not my dad. His face keeps changing as I get a good focus on him. How long have I been living in-here, in the back row? I look down at the contents of my bag. A real fire hazard, the contents have a neat way of self cleaning though. Snap! The bag is tidied up in a whirlwind, and settles onto my shoulders. "There!"

I feel a twinge of rage surfacing in my body, it curls up into a snake, and tightens in my belly. I am angry about the water!

"This is a list of what is in your water that comes from your faucet. Do not drink water from your faucet unless you have an extremely good filter. Here we simply have another means of "Culling the Population".

Fluoride
Chlorine
Mercury
Lead
PCB's

Arsenic
MTBE
DCPA
Perchlorate
Doxin
Hexachlorobenzene (HCB)
DDT" (4)

The rage curls into oblivion quickly, and my head swims over the crowd, curious of the conversation, my bag is tidied up and strapped on my back, and I'm on my way. My throat is sore from the cigarettes. I have a deep thirst, I can barely lumber over. (Tobacco invokes spirits.)

"Psst. Hey, Hey." I lean in, taking a long look at the two, they sit there, gorging on popcorn. A dark figure leans back in a cordial manner, resting her head on my shoulder so she may relax as she speaks to me, this is a comforting gesture, and it relaxes me.

"What are you guys talking about?"

"Sorry, we were just talking about this guy at work. He never stops falling off cliffs, it's just about how much better he is than everyone else, but he's going way too fast down the hill! He's got wings, his name, well I can't remember his name, can you hon?"

"No, I can't remember his name, no."

"Oh." I whisper. "Okay, I'm... Okay... I'm going to go get some water you guys."

"Okay." They both smile, one winks, and then they turn back to the screen chatting.

"I love him," I think I hear them say, and this sense of familiarity is helpful to calm me down about the water somewhat.

I go out to the godly foyer, neat candelabras burn low wax, a caped individual blocks his face from my glare, and passes me through the hall. We ignore one another. I just hear clicking shoes, and echoing, then finally say:

"Good day sir." Quietly under my breath.

"Don't notice me, I am not here, please move along!" The

man in the cape shouts, echoing his voice off of the walls. He will not say more, and I follow his instructions carefully, tiptoe down a long hallway, and down a set of carpet stairs, shivering.

I have the onset of a head cold, I can tell. I make my way to a crooked exit sign, it shorts out, I stumble backward through a door leading past thick, rubber curtains into a brightly lit cafeteria.

"Ah ha! Food, water! Yes." People mull about serving drinks, and cake and soda, and I adjust my eyes, at the birthday decorations hanging all around the room. It's more like a cold meat locker then a concessions stand, but they are selling things, I see. Super water! I hope it doesn't have ddt in it.

What am I wearing? A thick, woolen winter jacket, like a fox fur of some kind covers me. It's a good thing, because it is freezing (ass) cold in here. It even smells cold, how something can smell cold because it's frozen, and not hot.

A young, scrawny girl walks up to me from the theater, an asian girl, clutching herself tightly in her arms, attempting to keep warm in the nude. Why she's naked, I have no clue, but I feel bad for her anyway. I cordially say hello, and she has just woken up too. Her eyes squint, and she smiles.

"Hey!" She yawns.

"How are you doing?" The girl is a very attractive girl I'd say from Japan, but maybe she's Chinese or Mongolian, maybe even Indian, her face is clean, she yawns, she's tan, she shivers. I seem to know her from somewhere, so, I hug her with my big woolen coat, and pull her in so she's warm, wrapping her up, her skin is freezing cold, and jolts me awake, but I like it, and she laughs. We both laugh.

"Thank you, Aifreann." She says my name correctly, not like most people pronounce it, but like afid, the bugs who eat your plants and then you gotta spray cuz they chew 'em up real good. She says it how I pronounce it. and I just smile, and ask her how she knew.

"Wild story, it's a long one," she says.

"How long?"

"You'll see." We walk together from the half eaten vanilla cake on the table in front of us to go find water.

"My names Suki." She giggles.

"pretty name, Suki." I try to pronounce hers.

"su-ki, soooki, suki"

She laughs. I hope I'm pronouncing it right like she did mine. I feel warm now, like I'm floating in salt

"Let's go find some water." I say. Remembering my mission. Its urgency.

Near a concession stand I find a king cobra and an ice house beer, and some sodas, but no water. I pocket the beers, slipping the tall cans into my oversized coat pockets, and suspiciously look around. Suki pokes out her cute head, looking left, then right, then hiding back away. There are more people stumbling in from the movie theater, to grab concessions. At first they are fair, and cordial, but at some point, the crowd grows out of size, and violent, someone shouts:

"Its black friday!" And people stomp in from nowhere, crushing others under foot, the place twitches suddenly with bodies below bodies. We cross to a hallway under a buzzing EXIT sign, glowing neon green. I see a lady around ninety years old being trampled by twelve year old cheerleaders, and a woman with seventeen children, screaming.

"I can't watch this," I say, and have to look away. I watch other people opening the beers and looking around awkwardly, the girl is resting in the jacket holding on somewhere in there, as I make my way through the miserable crowd, delirious.

We find a hallway no one else sees, and take it out of the chaos, the bloody religious nightmare, consumption.

Through a fancy wine bar, we are circled around in a long loop, emptying to the outside.

I am stopped by a woman I have known before. I think she

12

is saying something about hunting rabbits, but I am not sure. I smile and the girl pokes her nose out, wiggling it. My acquaintance works as a bartender here at the wine bar, apparently.

"Hey!" I say, "I'm really thirsty, can I get some water?" I am shouting but everyone else in the bar is quiet, and looking at me.

"Of course, I'll get you some water!" She shouts back, winking at me. I watch her long black dreadlocks sway at her hips, back and forth as she procures the water. The audience in the bar avert their glances, and go back to eating.

"How have you been?" She says, once she is back. She pours a great big pitcher of ice water and then hands it to me.

"Oh, man would you look at this." Suki yawns, warmed up inside the jacket. She is now wearing my coat I gave her, and she looks incredibly attractive in it. Her tan legs poke out at the bottom.

"I'm thinking about hopping a freight train with this girl, she's never done it before." I say to my friend.

Suki sips the water and smiles.

"Or we can go to the town by the river," Suki says. "The waterfalls are there."

I smile at her.

"Well, I want to go." My friend says.

"I get off work in 10 seconds."

"Ten... nine... eight!." The three of us do a countdown and then leave the bar, me, giggling. Me, with a camping backpack on my back, then behind me, my friend with dreadlocks carrying Suki on her back, like a backpack. We are making our way along a steep Highway, using each others bodies by lying sideways and shuffling our hips side to side on the grass, having 'soft sex' to get up the hill, because, we figured out this is "smoothest, and softest."

"How long do you think till we make it?" Suki gets up, orgasming, and pants, stands there shaky like the deer. My friend stands, dusting herself off, and then brushing off the flecks of

13

grass from her vagina. She looks into the direction of the hills behind us.

"Sometimes I like to go this way when I get lost, some of my family lives up there." Suki says, pointing through the trees.

"Let's go try it." I say.

My friend shakes her head yes.

"Good we all agree."

I. A fire in the cemetery

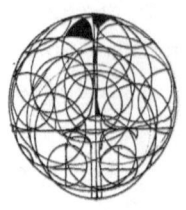

I want to talk about the first time I met Suki. Her image is slowly disappearing in my mind, and I fear I am forgetting completely. I try to imagine the details of her body, I cannot even imagine the details of my own right now. For so long I haven't thought about what I look like, it is frightening to think about even looking in a mirror. Do I have hair, young, or old, am I a woman or a man? Is my body a horse, or a mountain? In a dream, I saw my face melting when I looked at it in the mirror. My reflection at first sight was complete, intact, but slowly, it became elongated, and the skin sliced off my bones, exposed my fat. I could not recognize my appearance, and so to describe me, there it was.

I am, I gather, a consistently melting thing, evaporated at sight, smelling only of the remains of the room, surrounding the bones.

Suki must have learned to look past my appearance as a dead, slow apparition of waltzing bones, a single skeleton, warped away in some twisted and concise storm of a body.

We first made eye contact in one of those old-time-theater-gymnasiums, and she was shivering in her nude, and forgiving nakedness. I was standing in my fox fur coat, nested, looking down at my melting bodice out of some fear I may witness the sick folding of fat and skin like candle wax, dripping along my skeletal arms, I try to make up these details.

It may be, in fact, the hairs of my head mixed together with the molten skin and fat, and created the appearance of the fox fur, I don't know.

Where I am sitting now, there are cables plugged everywhere, holding me above the rushing waters below. I smell the labyrinth of rose and lavender on the banks. My skin is not melting now, intact, it is rosy, and glowing as under a lantern, there in the distance of willow trees, beyond.

I don't exactly recall ever even losing Suki in the first place, she just at some point had gone and evaporated into a memory, without my noticing, and with her, my dear friend who hunted rabbits, or she may have worked at a cafe, I am not clearly aware of much.

If I look back and view the past in one way, I get a set of dimensions, smells, pictures, props, and a clear image of what

I experienced at the time I am referencing now. When I look at the time tomorrow, I will see the scene almost completely opposite of today, as I am referencing the past, now. I will try again tomorrow.

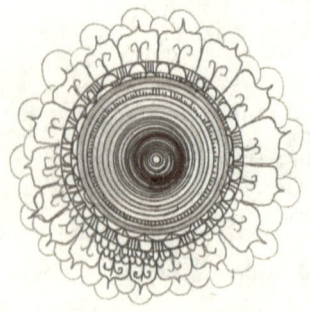

Suki and I met in a public park, I remember. She had this hat, a live cat, one of those all white cats, curled up on your head, sleeping.

I so wished to pet the beautiful cat, but Suki would slap my hand away every time I attempted such. She said it was a dangerous and highly disrespectful act to touch her white pussy cat.

I, instead, kept my eyes trained on her red lips, and saw as two orange fish swam back and forth inside of her mouth, as she spoke.

We were in the graveyard in Mehr, I remember now. Those cold and lonely March days seemed to unfold into forever, I had come to drop off roses for my grandmother, and to say a prayer over her. The sky was dark with thin grey looming clouds.

Taught inside my black suit jacket, frail, and boney in my skeleton outfit, hugging every groove of my bone structure, I must have seemed quite gaunt to her. I felt dead inside at least, to really keep me illuminated, whoa, this would take a number of flames, all going out in the wind, my soft warm light on the horizon used to call in all of the gnats, and fruit flies, but now this light had blown out.

"Where are you from?" Suki asked quietly, staring down at the wilted, black roses I had clutched neatly behind my back. As to not inform the sultry girl of my depression, and loneliness, I shivered silently, and looked down at the tips of my shoes, pretending to be only cold. My long suede leather shoes, without normal type string shoelaces, grew and grew; my feet, as it seemed, grew awfully large all of a sudden, as if I were some kind of clown, stuffed into cowboy boots warped with a brush.

I realized I had not looked at my feet before this moment, someone had dressed me, there was some kind of trickery. I also couldn't remember waking up this morning, and wondered what in the world this could mean. Yet, Suki's voice pulled me back out of the abyss of my shoes, and away from the snake skin of my growing thin boots.

"Excuse me, do you know how to get to the cemetery from here?" Her voice was tissue paper thin, hot in my grasp, milky and sunny, awkward, and surprisingly curious.

I looked up, and brushed my sadness from my jacket, offering her the black of the wilting roses.

"Come, we will go there together, madam. I offer this gift of my long heart." I held out the roses, all of its petals dropping, crackled dry, and watched her soft face under the great white cat, turn at the edges, into a smile.

We walked quietly, together, to my grandmother's gravestone, where I placed the blackened roses down in soft, white snow. All of the bones in my black suit leaning down upon the snow pack, I could feel my joints rubbing on the steel cold of the ice below.

When I had turned back to Suki, the rose I had given her lay at my side, the petals broken off in the white of the flakes. She was gone.

I knelt there, tears of warm salty liquid all drenched up and calm in my head. The cemetery was empty of Suki and her cat.

Standing up, dripping thoughts of Suki and grandmother out of my skin, it started up again. The feeling is like when you eat too many vitamins on an empty stomach, and for some it is like overheating in bed when you are sick, the nasty fire in the body, melting the flesh off the bones.

Standing in the middle of the graveyard in Mehr, as pedestrians passed by, I was clutching black roses on fire, as my whole body lit up, there melting in the rising flames, a bonfire in a black suit and tie; I stood, the bouquet held up in my right hand.

The melted version of me had passed, and I was all bone, no more suit, or flowers, just a skeleton. I sensed the call, and motivation to grow, and grow, taller, and taller, until I was lumbering at twenty feet in height. I made my way through the cemetery, using low willow branches to guide me, and searched every tomb and statue and stone for my beloved Suki, but the flames had brought me to my perfected body, I no longer needed her, the fire had mutated the brain, and calloused heart, drawing it out through tiny holes only bone can describe.

Mehr is a strange and lonely place when no one can see you. They rush about, seemingly unaware of the skeleton crossing avenues twenty feet tall in front of them, but, I, like the pace of the city, know my power. The tickle of those tiny people crossing me, toy taxi's bump over my toe bones. It tickles, and I try to stay away from Broadway avenue as much as I can. Usually, I stay in the parks, and watch the ducks pass by with their little boat bodies.

There's no knowing how much I consider time anymore, if I am down on Kook Island, I can simply keep track watching the Ferris-wheel, as it tics. It's easier to lumber around in this body down there on Kook Island, because the beaches are vast.

Someday -- I know -- I will have passed into the sand there, on one of those beaches, my bones will have warped away, and rattle on, shaved by the sands of time, fragile and brittle in the wind, the old lumbering skeleton gives away to the hatch of the heart, the new body will have been built from scattered trash I find while wandering. The place where my heart used to find refuge, a cavity is sewn around the spine, where I have placed a door.

When I turn into three different people, the girl, the child and the man, I always find myself standing next to a tree of a family home. I remember the living room of this house clear as crystal. The nineteen seventies was a time period of specific furnishings, there was a turn in decor, I remember it quite well. The issue I find, when I turn into three separate people, is I have no reference, there are three main voices, talking at once, as one spirit, all broken up. So, if I remember a memory based in the nineteen seventies, I must have lived there, how would I know the place otherwise? Being the way I am now, I am from a different time period, two thousand years into the future; so, I could insist my memory is flawed in some way from the split, when I become dream, but I know I'm invisible to everyone around me, although when I look in the mirror, I see myself. My skin is pale, paperwhite, my eyes are missing, and two black spirals have replaced them. Behind me, there is a couch, where a shadow moves across the room. My skin begins falling off, and I have to turn away. The others, they cannot see me, but I can see them.

If you go back in time, and think of a simulation, a text, you will come up with a new environment altogether. Even when the story is right in front of you, the simulation, and you are reading the text, new visions will come into your mind, some based on the day, some based on your current emotion.

Frangible, fragile and brittle; my lungs erode, made of trash collected along the beaches of Kook Island, and a dark red glob falls to the sand. A new consciousness lays its pearl sheen; the old skeleton slowly buried in the sand. My old skull peeps out to say goodbye. Its high tide, the ocean washes over the glob of pearl being, pulling it on string to the mouth of the water. The salt rinses off the purple latex, and cleanses the grooves of the new body, while the sun goes down on the horizon, and then the moon and stars come out.

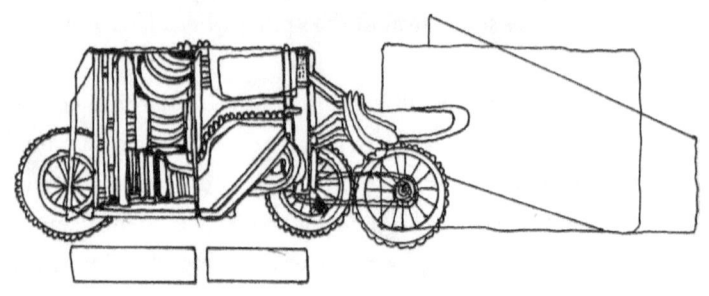

My Grandpa's
Space Station Channel

I stroll down the elevators, stale bodies tied to the walls -- I may need to illuminate some of their mutterings. I use a new guava fruit as an interpreting device here, decode and translate pressed to ON. Stubborn languages I have to take out, take apart, photograph with this here trusted camera, snapshots of the larva hidden on the lips. The guide had taught us well, which body for which time period, the way we could enter and leave, the way we could disintegrate, multiply, she taught us how to care for ourselves, how to love, and also how to roam.

The smell around the transistors (may they be considered, multiple offenses under these new nostrils) merely a door into another environment, and there are many doors here; in the body, in the mind.

The elevator opens on the 25th floor, some of the bodies unhook from the walls, leave, and some bodies drag their feet, enter. Today is my first adventure into the "lower spine," as the guide calls it. Which is literally where I have been holding onto anger and sorrow. She is helping me release it in this new simulation called the Lower Spine.

Almost seems like they move with each of my breaths, these zombies.

The flies piss me off~ though, I have to say. Now we're moving. The lift rises, and we are sent as an unformed group, through TV segments, these commercial lands, of the color version, new and improved!

Last week was the black and white TV, now were spun into (at last) our "show bodies." Our names are on every shelf in the entire universe, even the local grocers carry us, our faces on the package, the bodies on the elevator, they are the ones I am looking at, those things, gross, fly eaten parts of me. With little adds around us for mashed potatoes, and pepper, I think the smell got to be too strong, I'm guessing.

People at home right now are lined up at their dinner trays, watching this show, in this elevator, and they are eating mashed potatoes out of a box. Grandpa, and Suzanne, And no name, and the other no name, they are all representative of myself in a different time period.

I am in the den, with my Grandpa, eating mashed potatoes with pepper, and looking around and seeing me on the elevator, the "me" there is in the future.

I take another direction, a different air. I look' at the carpet; the many pre-designed flowers woven there.

I watch now, the cracks in the elevator filled with ants and flies and caterpillars~

"Forget the feathers in the stairway," R(ei)ka Whispers. "Just

21

view the lake from above." I look out the glass wall at the lake. The elevator goes up, and I see the tower over the lake. They have been building something there. I see a new escalator to the top of the place, and I watch as people jump into the water from way up.

A sample of simulated present entanglement. The number three was taught in classes as if it were the number two in pre-school~ So, now when I go to the toilet, I am going number three or number five, not number two.

Must be all fucked up, for people who learned number two before number three, what in the fucking hell is wrong with those people?

But, I am with the children from floor #2, and they learned number four was number one.

Where is Suki? I ask someone. The kid looks up at me, as I dial his floor number. He is crying because he says, he is lost.

"I am confused really bad." The poor little dude sobs.

"It's okay, dude, you are me, I am you, I am confused, were gonna be okay, because… Wait, what am I saying…" I stop, rub my chin, all the kids are staring at me silently.

"Have you guys seen a kid named Suki running around?"

I imagine a thief lingers in the leaves. I ignore all of the children loudly boarding the elevator and press the button for floor 75000, 60053 as Gramps eats some mashed potatoes and drops a bit on his TV dinner tray … He smiles over at me, his dentures hanging there.

"Gramps, I'm really confused, and scared." I cry.

"I spilled." He says and eats it off the tray. Juicy brown bits of steak and sauce floating around in his gums between the dentures.

I hold up a random thing I must have been holding. A circuit board in my hands; I wrap my fingers loosely around it, and hold it up to my chest.

Where is Suki? I mutter, shivering.

Gramps just grumbles and turns up the TV.

We hear a bird in the chimney, and Grandpa mutters and turns it down, grumbling, he sits up slowly.

My sister laughs, sitting perched next to me.

"Who's Suki?" She says.

On the TV rockets take off through the screen. I am feeling a fever, as I board a rocket in my spacesuit, my sister and grandpa wave from the crowd in the TV We Ride-on, injected with stamina, me and a chimpanzee, named Susan. This place, in-here is a blob of origami, the way they made the walls. I see me in my helmet from my TV dinner tray as a kid, watching through my tears.

"He's got a monkey, Grandpa." My sister shouts.

"Huh?" Gramps is fiddling with something in the fireplace.

I ride around in cartoon circles around the globe twelve times in an origami rocket across a painted on canvas background of space. In the show, I take off my suit and board the elevator, to the bottom of the ship. This time the elevator operates using skateboards, powered by yelling and shouting actresses, and pulleys. Everyone breaks out in song and dance, holding flower pots, doing line dancing routines on the ship, everybody's dressed in cowboy outfits.

The origami rocket passes around the moon sixteen times. Circles the earth four times, and the children from floor 2 board the roller coaster ride from floor #2 to join the parade. They hold up big red circles above their heads, and shout things like "We want a cookie we want a cookie and Free the monkey, Suzanne is our friend!"

They want to touch the red dots in their vision. I remember wanting to do the same.

Above us, onboard, the waterfall of our mysterious ancestors cover the rocket; this is what the guide tells all of the new passengers. The ship keeps circling, and circling until we all get very nauseous. I hang upside down with my monkey Susan, eating our dinner out of my hat. I ask her if she's seen Suki, and the monkey hands me a banana.

Grandpa climbs outside, with a kid in the yard. It is "Me," a long time ago. We climbed into the old tree, the tree in our yard with the human fingers, and he showed me how to get around it, along-it, the tree uses these little fingers, he'd say, to lift up kids To where they belong. Grandpa and I planted the tree together the day after Christmas and grandpa showed me how to plant the roots, bury em deep, and water them.

Through beads and ribbons and rivers of jar lids with pink string, Image and light thoughts and internal perspective A train-boat passes overhead in the city, closely followed by an alligator, carrying an umbrella, shouting about being late to the prom.

"He must be young." I think. "Looks old enough to me."

Grandpa Says, holding my arm in his grasp.

"In the future, they're gonna invent a boat to fly."

I say to grandpa. "One like a train in the sky."

Grandpa goes quiet after a while, real quiet.

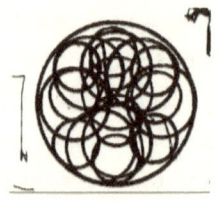

A shaded grove leads the three of us down along a ravine, into an open field, where we pause, lost, watching the forest sway in the wind. I see it first, then Suki, then my friend whose name I can't remember. An old blue ford rumbles out of a shaded grove into the middle of the path before us, sticking the gears, and grinding, the rusted wheels tear up clods of mud, and it spins out.

"There's no driver...There's no one driving the car." I say, touching my friends shoulder briefly. She sees it too. The ford stuck sideways down there in the mud, she focuses her eyes, squinting.

"Yeah, it's crazy, no one's driving the car, what the fuck?" Suki just laughs.

"Come on you guys, Billy's insane, we don't want to talk to him." She pulls us away from the ravine, straggling behind her.

"But where is he? I don't see anyone." I say as she shuffles me along forward.

"You don't want to see him, believe me." Suki says. As we leave the ravine, more trucks pull up, and get stuck down there in the mud.

"What in the hell?" I mutter. Suki leads us to an old hut made out of branches, and steps up to a handmade platform being used to serve drinks on. Inside of the hut hangs a delicate looking basket where normally a server might stand. The basket is lowering in minuscule drops, the way a spider lowers when it spins to the ground.

"Is R(ei)ka here?" Suki says to the basket.

"Who are you talking to?" My friend wonders.

"Just a moment, R(ei)ka!"

Our guide, R(ei)ka, tells us of the origins of time. She sits us down, and whispers songs into our memories. I didn't yet understand time, what it was, or who built it, but the song she sang illuminated something inside of me. I'm still not quite sure what.

R(ei)ka walks us down a long thin path, next to the river, where we cross into an old, deep forest. Suki giggles, and my friend, excited, tramps along, bouncing at the beat of a song I will never know.

"Of 'ye olden times," the guide teaches

"We were a class of millions, all fish in a school of thought, stronger, and smarter together." I watch her misty body dissolve around the edges of these words, as she expands and contracts,

25

a fine particle of moisture, appearing, then dissolving away.

"When we arrived," she teaches, "we were equipped with our new bodies. These bodies had been lived inside for many years before we came along. And Although used, our new bodies being much like rentals, we could transcend or descent." Evaporating, R(ei)ka comes back up to us on the path, holding up a loofah bar.

"If we ever get stranded alone in the forest," she says, "suck on the water, by soaking a loofah in the Earth, Like this." She bends down and rubs the loofah into a small puddle in the moss. Suki watches intently, and my friend takes notes in her journal. I am giggling secretly to myself.

"Yes, I see." Suki says now and then.

"First, now drop it over your lips." She gives a brief demonstration, and a little blonde child around the age of five appears next to her, tries it, and then disappears just as fast. The thin liquid comes out of the sponge, and settles at R(ei)ka's lip edge. I'm giggling, but no one cares, or notices.

My friend, whose name I cannot for the life of me remember, with the dreadlocks stands over me, with the loofa, dripping it into her mouth. She grows as the water pools in through her lips, five then ten, then twenty inches taller than before.

"What is this?" I say, curious. With her waving, curly black hair in an aline haircut, the dreadlocks come away.

"Your hair changed." I try and say. She just ignores me, and continues drinking.

Suki doesn't seem to notice anything either. Her hair is cut at her neck line. She smiles watching Suki drink from the loofa.

I bend down in the moss, and trying to dip the sponge I found into a small puddle of gathered water, my hands won't function, I am struggling to grip the loofa.

I look on, trying to focus, blurring my eyes behind our guide, where I see a giant dog with the head of a man crossing behind the girls. Roughly, the monster creeps through the fog on a trail north. The animal is the size of a bear, and is looming slowly towards us.

"What is this?" I shout, dropping the loofa. Our guide turns and looks, and then chuckling, explains to us it is an outlaw and it is one of our friends here.

She asks us to get closer and the three of us, child and mother, and I (still clutching the dripping loofah bar) walk to the wolf halfling, terrified and shivering.

As we get closer, the thing changes, from half dog to human being, now dressed in a bowler's hat with a vest and a pocket watch and a chain, a man from the early 1800s.

"This is Albert. He is a werewolf, he is also an inventor." R(ei) ka Says, holding up her hand in a bow.

With a smoky grin, Albert describes to us his origins, and ideas about animation. Excitedly, he describes his animation process to us, and I look over my shoulder and notice there are model cars parked along the road.

"Hey, Billy's coming." I say, tapping Suki's shoulder, trying to get her attention.

"By the model I would say the year is 1975." Albert interrupts, saying. I look over my other shoulder and notice a small, rectangular card flyer, where the cars were. The card describes a concert in a crawl space, somewhere outside of East London. The card has been placed before me on a table. The first has evaporated away.

I pick up the card and inspect its detail, and without my notice, I am transported to the crawl space, and the sound slowly catches up to my ears.

I'm in East London, in an elongated tunnel in an attic, I see others in the audience behind me, in front of me, and all around me. A girl with long liberty spikes in her hair DJs two records simultaneously, all from the late 1970s. I look around for the guide but see her nowhere. I look for Suki, and my friend, but they aren't there either. I shift around the room, three times and try to dance, but my body won't do this, so I just relax and let the music peel me down.

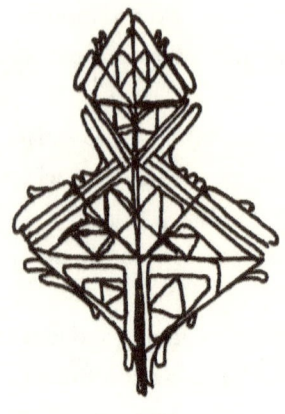

In Larva (Circa 2534) Bags of 'fillet o' fish' hang on the front door of the house, I'm followed closely by a shadow, I'm walking up Main Street. I see each certificate within twelve arms, planted in the middle of the road, grown out of the torso, they climb the apple blossom. I read one, but it's in gibberish.

"A blob loses fat and becomes paper-origami down the street." it says. I throw the paper down. I see there's a thief, hiding in the leaves, and pull out a spray can, and an eight percent beer, crack it open; a cat jumps across the street to the sound, chk-sht! wrapped in circuit boards blinking little lights, reflecting casts over the gutters, puddled rain and a blue and green flickering light.

I cross, and approach with my spray can aimed at the thief - Thief with Chimney rockets, feverishly on stamina, if you know what I'm saying here - I Approach shouting flower pots. Red dots in my vision arrive out of place, reflections of the puddles, the crossing cat, and arrive in front of the Willow tree, hanging dinners out of my hat.

I offer some to the thief as bait. He thinks about it for a moment, eases back and forth, hanging there in his shadow, and declines with a gesture-

"You've stolen my friends dear sir, Suki, and the girl, I can't remember her name..."

He begins climbing into his Willow tree, as himself, but younger than he appeared before, as a kid, I'm in his yard. He's aiming his wrist rocket at me.

"Don't shoot!" I shout, ducking beneath my arms for cover.

I hang my fingers with beads and ribbons and jar lids with pink shoe string, drooping. At my feet is my new body, dressed in her finest suit.

"Oh, another one," She lies there sleeping sound. {One squishy reptile enters over my vision of her on a screen before me, and an audience of three in all, we lounge back watching the movie in this dark smoke filled movie theater.

"Hey, guys I had a weird dream or something, Was I sleeping?" I hear my voice saying this to the two next to me. This vision begins to erode, brittle, like a wafer chip, it starts to crumble away and is gone.}

I walk in my new stale bodies, there is three of me now: the thief, the girl, and the child. Illuminating the old house, we approach with flashlights, the dark living room windows with curtains.

"Suki? Is it you," I say to the child, who giggles, but it doesn't look like Suki.

"Hey, what's your name, is it you there?" I say to the child.

He just laughs, and makes a funny face, by pulling his lips apart in a crude manner, and sticking out his tongue.

"Blahhhh." The child spits.

Hidden new languages surface between us after four minutes of me trying to communicate with the child, the girl, and the thief.

We pass a Guava fruit back and forth between us, and begin to learn whispering commands.

I, as my female self, the girl began to illuminate the transistors with my flashlight, once in the basement of our old house. The furniture is reminiscent of 1975. My flashlight beams are everywhere I look, because I can cross between all three sets of eyeballs, very awkward at first, but it starts to get easier, and smooths out as we enter each room. We are searching the shadows as they reach out from the concrete walls of the basement. We enter the body closest, in each breath, there is a door opening and closing, it is very uncomfortable to split into three individuals, I'll say. A possession, where the eyes turn cold white, and the muscles begin running autopilot, a possession from a spirit who wants to play baseball, is how I would describe it.

When we enter the basement for the third time, we see feathers rise from below the floor, through the pipes in the house, from the plumbing, from under our feet, and into a stairway. We follow the feathers down to another room, and when we arrive, the lake comes flooding us out, and up to a tower higher in the neighborhood, up on the hillside.

I know this is a sample of a simulated present entanglement, one of which I've heard about studying consciousness with our guide years ago. She had told me to relax, as I ride on the cold lake water, upward.

I didn't know what it meant at the time, but now, as I experience it, I am glad to have met her those many, many years ago.

The Televisions spin on TV dinner trays beside us, and I grab ahold of the child, and the thief.

"The sky will fill with ants." The guides voice whispers. "And the water will crash you into a tower."

When the three of us get inside the tower, the floor has been freshly wood stained, and there is a guitar playing in the middle of the room, building furniture from its songs. A bed pours through a speaker, like liquid chocolate. A table and chairs, and Violin pours through the speaker into a basin of white china. A golden trumpet melts out, landing down in the room. And the girl and the thief and I sit at the table, and play on the instruments, and dine with the guide herself.

Guide: "When you look up into the light with your eyes, witness the settling chairs, your majesty, the brain."

She stirs a glass of liquid slowly as she speaks.

"In its clothing case," She points at the dresser, "It animates, with its lobster tail shadows, keeping up behind it. In the helium balloon, in their pyramid, our dusty crumbs of life, become our magic, our power. She smiles, a smirk, and Evaporates for a while.

Landing wings down, our guide becomes a large bird, perched onto a nightstand.

"Of fish fry onto the edges of the rocks ~This is where, in landing, I find the half specimen of leak-latched-doors to the caves near the sea~" She disappears again, evaporating completely.

Alabama Billy

When I go to the grocer, I notice the Velour tablet resembling chalk (half-life) behind my swollen tongue. I have been living as a lost child in the Moony age. In my image of myself, I have strapped a tightened mouthpiece to my jaw, a paste around the edge of my mouth. Hungry, I am walking through the grocery store, viewing all of the hash brown patties best to worst. Different companies like Heinz, and then you got your "no name brands" … I'm staring at these hash browns, when a litter of pigs surrounds me, following my every move. At my feet, the farrow doesn't want to leave my side, So, I start feeding em hash browns and apples off the shelves. I fear I will trample the poor things if I move wrong. Plus, I keep asking them if they knew someone named Suki because I miss her, but you know, nothing, no response. I really miss her.

Rubbing my eyes, I swallow the small Velvet dose of Velour, and my heartbeat is heard as the decibel of sounds in the grocers raise to a size of a voluptuous female giant-{Amber, rose, concentric circle, gold, pine-needle-blanket. I arch upon my fleeting mood, drifting in a southern wind through Virginia}, {carried on the ants, who crawl through the pine needles down the road, I arch back.} the ride leads down along a ravine, into a forest, into an opening. I see an old blue ford parked in the mud there. Across my path, on the other side, I see a double-headed baby tiger in the desert, half of its body is a deer, wobbling across the deserted streets of New Mexico - I turn back and see the old ford stuck in the mud, and remembering what Suki had said about Billy, I chose the dessert, and take off in its direction, pulling on the ants, who walk me.

A dude with a shaved head walks passed me.

"Hello." They say, holding up a waving claw where their hand used to be.

My mouth hangs open from the sight of the double-headed deer/tiger. The dude pushes my jaw back up.

"You know staring is rude right?"

"Yes, Oh, sorry," I say.

"I'm looking for a friend of mine."

"Oh yeah? Who might it be?" he says snarkily.

"Her name's Suki. Have you met someone by the name?"

"Can't say I have, ain't no Asian folk I know of in the town of Billy?" he spits.

Brown cud strings down off of her lips cracked and worn.

I choke up.

"Billy?"

"She's not Asian per se, she changes Forms?"

"Forms? What the hell is this supposed to mean, forms?"

"You know, bodies," I say, kinda scared now.

"Like a Body snatcher?" he chuckles, then turns serious.

"We got plenty of those around here, being as we are in the town of Billy, but you shouldn't be looking for them, they eat your soul, they will." he spits again.

We saunter into the deserted town bar and lumber off six rounds of whiskey straight, no chaser. I'm proud of my accomplishments but begin to forget where I am, and I am led by an old gentleman, down along the tracks to where they say Tyranny lives.

"I gotta get going." I try and say, but they don't hear me. I can't tell if it's the heat waves or whiskey, but everything starts to look steamed, fuzzy, and blurry. I try to offer driving a car, try, but I almost wreck it somewhere behind an alleyway, and no one wants me to drive. It's all I remember.

Later, I'm at the same bar again, maybe the next day, or maybe it was next week, I'm drawing in the girl's bathroom; and someone's in there with me for some reason, looking at me in horror, as I draw a heart so perfect, so, my friend, Suki might see, and know I'm here.

"If she were ever to pass through this deserted old town in the desert, she'd see my heart," I mutter to 'em.

"We're gonna have the heart removed." They say, "And get down to scrubbing it off if you know what's good for ya."

Woken up by dad, I get up, he leaves for work, and I walk out to the train tracks, near Sherries. Dad is an old bum who used to ride freights, he lets me settle in at his house sometimes when things get rough, and let me tell you they do. He and I play guitar, and we get to drinking and singing up a hollerin' storm, almighty!

I'm all hungover, walking to Sherries, when I see his face, confused, looking out the truck sideways at me. I just wave a hand and see him driving. He doesn't have time to stop. I wave, but he doesn't have time.

At Sherries, I meet the dude, and his three punk friends with purple, black, and green mohawks, who tag along, silently.

After we eat and smoke cigs and drink cups of coffee, they offer I come to their house, mentioning something about Suki being there.

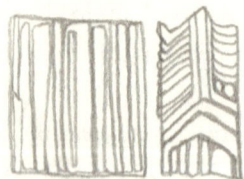

So, excited, I walk with them through the deserted town, passing abandoned hotels, across the old train tracks, long out of commission.

We all see the two-headed baby deer crossing the abandoned streets. The deer's one head bobs down and lifts a little after camouflaging behind its body, to reveal another head, a baby bobcat, and then a tiger cub.

Tyranny says: "At the festival, women made toy men out of sticks, and Hominids would gather by the river. They made the toy stump along with the sticks and they'd attach their hands, they would.

"What?" I say.

"The Year 1323." Tyranny says.

The sadness of God shows up on televisions nearby. "Lingering clouds and lies for sale!"

Beyond the train tracks, God comes aboard a freight train and laughs, smiling at us. The freight train bends around a corner in the words hooked to a boat, in the sunrise. The words say BILLY in big, red letters.

On this boat, God is carrying a box of keys … A loud siren heats up and spins away behind the train, and dust patterns up on my shoulder and neck, devouring any recognizable sound, my ears are devoured, and the siren hunts the deserted land for secrets, I guess, blaring down yonder.

"This Land once served the booming industry, all wasteland, and ghosts now." Tyranny says.

"All those working-class, all them infested with us half breeds, all our shadows wander-in' all this priceless interstate, just wastelands, threatening extinction!" Our group of punks hung their heads, letting this sink in a while as we walked.

We passed sidewalks of shattered booze bottles, and cigarette packages littering the back alleys.

"This supermarket, forty years ago, a memory." Tyranny says to us.

"It sometimes runs its fingers through my mind, a dusty hand grabbing the shelf of objects, a form now folded away and boarded."

"The cellophane removed and rotting meat beneath caked with maggots. And they talk about hell, well kids, here it is, the

35

wasteland of consumption. Billy"

I could feel my memories sewing back together as they spoke, deeply the long needle, punctured through the fabric, and ran a thin thread.

When I come to, my long sleeve shirt is there, khaki, I am now viewing it within a trance, not allowing myself to look away. There are Bats swooping over my head. I hear them. It is night in the desert, and tyranny and the punks are gone, no Suki.

I am blissed out, probably they drugged me, I am waiting for a reaction, my shirt to move or talk, so I can feed the paranoia grapes. I sit up all night and then walk back to dad's house, lonesome.

They shave the yard away, the orange dead creates dust; I put on my handkerchief over my neck and press it over my face, as a simple sawing away of clovers, and shivering of machine blades clumsy, cuts at the nasty heart and stones fly.

We grow infinite embers and chambers at this moment as I wait in my squat, boarded up three-story house along the old train yard in East County. Dad left for work an hour ago.

Every house on the block is empty or used mainly for drugs, flop, sex, I figured what the hell, I'll squat.

Less Rosemary grows these days along the tracks.

Terry, the old boozehound lumbers past the window drinking his 40 oz., he spits violently, like blood, like he was hit hard, and spits it with such a violent gesture, he's saying: I am stronger than you. He and I met at the local soup kitchen; we've been hanging out for years now since the day they dosed me.

The coins in my pocket I fidget with, drop one out of my pocket and watch it hit the wood floor. This signals Terry. He stops and turns to the squat. My heart is black and white houndstooth.

Snowfall of brown grass slowly crosses the street from the yard and lands on Terry. Soft, intricate, he handles the flakes of grass, wiping them off, and walking up to the front door of the squat from the sidewalk. I sit, reading the lexicon in the living room in my mask, he's banging on the door.

"Come in, I shout." After the fifteenth knock. He stumbles over the tres and puts his hand out with the beer.

"Here," He foils and stumbles at the nail poking sideways at the entrance. I laugh. He releases violence but keeps the beer stable through it.

He is a very carnal individual. He has symptoms I will have to process later. I feel like I'm losing breath, so I take off the mask and chug some beer of his. Goodness threads over me, like vines, through me like passageways of the red light rolled gently into a dryer full of shoes and boots and clogs.

I burp.

I met a girl named Suki today. He says.

The beer flies out of my mouth, and I jump up from the dirty couch, my lexicon flying.

"Where?!" I shout, chugging the beer. The ace, Terry is dancing now, his hair flies, helping by twisting his knotted jaded body into ladders sideways, and adhering mirrors to his chest from the wall in my living quarters, and aiming the light of the sun out of the door.

"Where what?" He says, snickering and demanding his beer.

"Where did you meet the girl?"

"You know, Suki! Like you said."

His leather boots with no souls left, he spins, and I hand him back the beer half finished, half full. He pours license plates into his giant mouth, singing the gargled liquid of a small orange cat into the air, and the cat comes by, landing from the balcony, on the steps, and wanders inside.

We act like we're having a shootout in a western, or were under the water, our blond hair swimming through the room, and blending into the cat, in a purple blur of silk.

"I never said anything about no Sooki." He says finally.

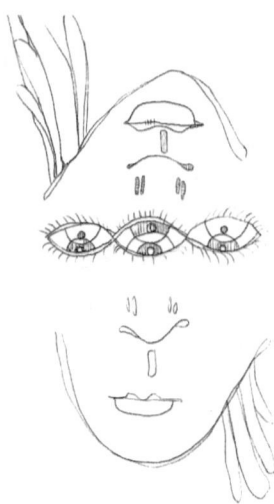

The three of us turn our bodies into a shaped fire, our feet are bent in the fusion, above a list of looping belt buckles (our water stilettos,) wherein cigarette smoke (with the cat) we cross beaver dams of hat, dimension to the front of my morning with the Velour tabs, and I am sitting on the couch, and I see Terry is turning his body into the cats. And I'm lit on fire, and it is starting up the couch.

The flame burns out into the grey sky - My skin melting. A shape of fire I've somehow forgotten about the skin ignited in me. The old fireplace, love is. I'm petting the cat "Terry" drinking my 40 oz.

I'll be honest, I first started feeding Terry a year ago in the backyard, when he was a skittish alley cat, now floating under clouds in my three-story house, I light the cats hair up a little and try to blow it out. In the sky, in my sandwich of Terry human, and Terry kitty cat, alley cat, what's the difference if I really walked to the store for the 40, and imagined Terry?

The cat's fire goes out. In my head, white statues are silent, perched there. Figures, marble. The rain starts tapping at the roof while I pet the cat. I roll up a cigarette and light it with my melting finger. I think I'm hearing Honking trains at a floating station, somewhere, southern drawl turning down the tracks, but those lines have been abandoned for years. Riding around in my living room, drunk as a skunk on my bicycle, I feel I'm reaching math, hours later. I'm learning the sleight of hand.

The 40 is gone, the cat's now playing in the string on the couch.

I list the surfaces in the squat: White, aluminum, wood, American flag, pink native string. I ride around the squat, sipping the 40. My bike has a loose chain. The smell reminds me of earlier when I lit on fire, the smell of everything in the room but me. I go back to focusing on the sound outside, the sawing of the grass, they are attempting to clean up the neighborhood, the sawing enters my mind, buzzes the statues, the instructions lying on a sheet of paper, next to the statues:

"Prior to leaving your pencil costume on the floor, you mentioned that you could postmark four of your personality aspects, and ship them, with our help of a compass, and four batteries, mirror thermos, cameras that you would help us braid the Izzy belle necklace. Thank you for understanding, Yours,

The Think feast." The voice is familiar, but I can't remember her name, oh yeah... R(ei)ka,(time) the guide, or something like this. I try to remember. Sudden, quiet, full of stars, the zodiac nest, believed, and gathered, undressed and blanketed: no insistent sawing, please no insistent sawing

I peek out the window and see the man in orange, bloody, lying in the street silent. I sit back on the couch. His saw is running, it seems he cut himself and is dead. My 40 oz. is full again, and capped.

Serves him right, you ain't never gonna clean up this neighborhood. I'm starting to like the town of Billy, never thought I'd say it.

39

The cat releases Terry, spitting up a hairball mixed with him onto the wood floor.

"Blech!"

"Blech!"

"Blech, Blech!"

"Yuck!" I shout.

Terry coughs up a small two-headed deer in puss on the wood floor, and nurtures it, shivering in the hairball of slime, and the cat's hair covering him. I give the baby deer a blessing, saying:

"Instruments along your legs, merging you in winding Lattice, gypsy vines entangle flutes, your name's wind! Your names wind!"

The shivering deer wobbles to life and wanders around the squat, one head decides one way, the other head decides the opposite.

Terry collapses from the traumatic birth to the floor. The cat sneaks into my bedroom. I crack my fresh 40 and guzzle it.

The

  Sawing

    Starts

Back

Up

        Out

side.

"I run my bloated, drunk fingers through the mossy curtain and watch the orange suit mowing the lawn, cutting through nettles.

I see the tongue, and heart of this town being removed.

"At least I got this hair-of-the-dog-beer," I think, chugging.

"Just watch him like a swaying tablecloth, move your hair out of your eyes." Staring at the man like he's on a monitor, my eyes polka dot ~"

Siberian Tigers

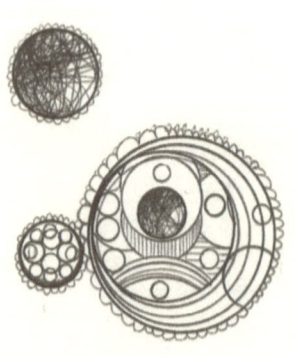

I am floating along the highway, on a blow up green inner tube -Madame, sir- head first, with my feet behind me, I cruise on my floaty, taking turns, watching for big Ford trucks from the other direction, and they're slowing down for me to pass.

"I am Suki!" I shout, curling along the highway on my green floaty.

I will inform you, madam & sir, on my arrival to Kook Japan, I found a monkey's house, way down deep in the forest. I found her cooking was sub psychedelic with a little sprucing up ...er...whoops... scratch it ... I found her earlier, cooking food, and she allowed me to change my outfit and even shower while doing so.

"Suki," she would say, "You are too friendly to be stinking up a storm." This is the day I found a black and white snail in my right nostril, in Kook Japan. I had tried so hard, with my pointer finger and thumb to wiggle the awful thing out, and pull it (maybe even ripping it) out of the crevasse in my nostril; but, the thing would not let up, and kept sucking back in there. It continues living in there to this day! Surely, this must disturb, or even entertain you miss / sir I don't know. It's been living in there, sir / madam / cat / octopi / Rushki / wah-wah / you you / floating in a car down the road of my insides for weeks, and according to the dream journal I have kept, the 3rd gear shifter isn't working properly and the car must not drive alone, so the snail is needed? I am confused. We must clear this up at once, dear.

The car I drove was an Oldsmobile, and now I use a floaty from the swimming pool, but anyway, the Oldsmobile must have looked like a swerving canoe on wheels, so logically I parked, and took to the swimming spot next to the side of the road. The Deep green waters ran over the Fallen trees. The massive Fallen oak trees were peopled with people, standing on the trunks, diving into the water...

Anyway, someone looked at me as I approached and I think I tried to swim, but I cannot remember?

Kisses, Suki.

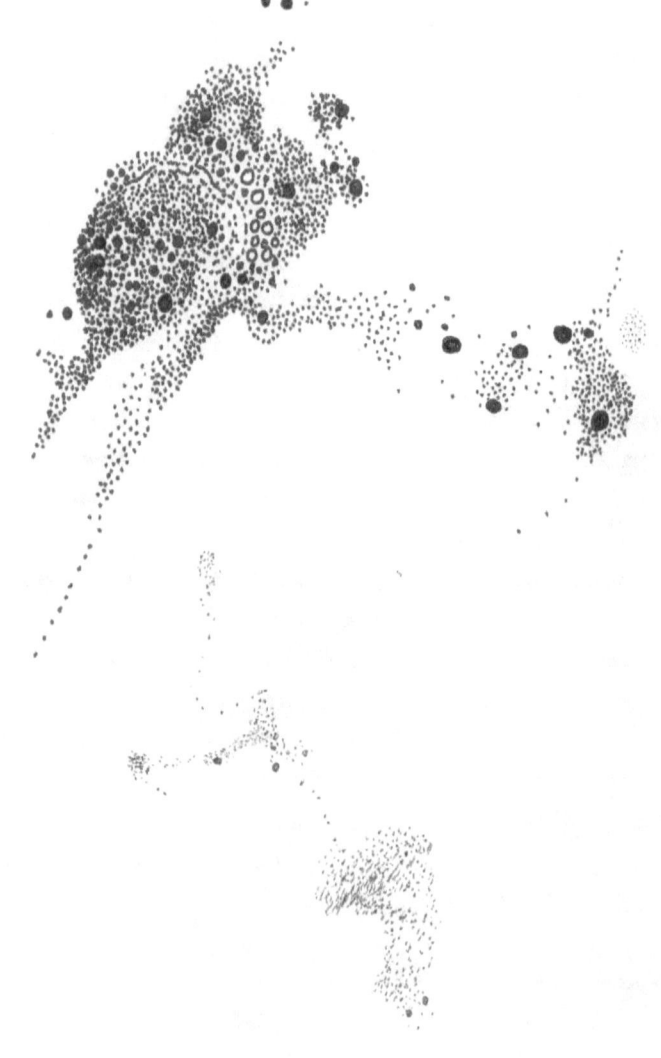

1543

My "form" comes undone. I am miserable inside of these many trappings. I built this 'here township. Various, I am sitting at the saloon, spitting chewing tobacco, piano playing. Snake eyes lands on the dice bar. Though I continue working my hands, slumped over, something' awful. I constrict the cards, rolling them, sweaty. I do these little experiments with my hands, I'd call it, but it's just fancy talk, I feel tortured, maintained in this exquisite posture.

My ten gallon hat, and snakeskin boots with trench coat sweaty'r 'an hell in a bat museum, yes sir. And my balance is all off, I feel like they could see me through the cards: aces, all four, in my hand. The skull and crossbones laced up nice in front of me, all four of them, printed down on these cards.

I'm terrible at bluffing, I'm not a lying type, rather be real, and witness, but I do lie at times. Dust off the sleeves, mid winter out there, waitress pulls back the curtains, and ties 'em up, and I see the collapse, all the snow piled high. At the loss of another failed harvest. Summer went by, then by again. And here we are.

Jackal laps up some beer, and shoots a stink eye at me. He spits over the spittoon, and it misses, long slime, black like his eyes is black. I spin my glass, and try to relax with them all looking harsh at me, drunk, miserable, smelling fools.

"Lass, bring me on down another beaker of emptiness, would yah, darlin?" I take a tall sip off the whiskey, and slam back a sarsaparilla to chase her. I am rife with intoxication.

I light up a smoke, and let the house smooth out, the table shivers a bit, as I throw in another chip, and then Jewel, and then the other two, and in my torrential downpour of sweat, I shake off the trench and pocket the cards, before nobody notices.

Abigail comes back with our drinks, and I follow the glass to the table, the shadow it leaves on the pocket chips and the folding money, and the six shooter which haunts me, with its curling fine edge, the sword of the west, glowing, the old curly cues, and those flower decorations mean death, not beauty.

So, why the trick, I wonder, laying down my cards. The room shuffles, underfoot. Something big under the ground breaks through it, all splintered and torn up right below the sheriff, and the bastard who tried to took my girl. And the bank man, they alls swallowed up under the saloon, screams of nightmarish fear make me feel sumpin' for 'em, but it's just human.

"Perversions of the spirit!" -The priest shouts from the up stairs with Reida clutching tight his tiny cross, and holding it against the creature emerging there in the center of the room. I sit here stunned, watch old Jewel get up shooting, and I grab my pistol, from the card table, and start shooting too. Taking another tincture of homemade tonic, Abi is screaming, and Bob is on there riding the awful thing like a horse buck wild.

"YOOO HAW!" He's shouting, lassoed up, and spinning something quicker than a bull or any old horse. Something so fast, the spaces in-between the lightning speed are all I see. I turn in torment from the depths of this being before me, and shout something I learned from Sasuke, the native shaman boy who let me live with him when I was dying of demons. [Shatuasa!] I hurl me out the winder so hard, I can't imagine how I'd not make it, but there's only so much allowed. Only the sadness of life, the real down darkness , really stops you from getting through a salty old saloon window. The castle spinning through the bar hammers in our collective nightmare. The stones crushing the place into flat. I feel the cuts in my body, and in my clothes, and pull myself up, and run. Wobbling, my blood trailing behind me, and knowing she could systematically Angel Cleanse my whole faculties, really swoop down, and do my life damage, I know its a healing coming, in my faculties.

I undress in the middle of the road, people coming out of they homes, my nausea is thick, and I puke up the whiskey, strong, and blur, my eyes are blind by the retching, and I chug back an old form, my pocket Vodka. Pure. No chaser. It burns good, and I pour it over my body, and hold up my arms like Sasuke taught me.

I choke the last of the vodka down, and spit on myself for not being able to handle the flavor.

"Christ, for eleven days I've hunted for my true love, and here she is, and I can't even handle a sip, Here baby!" I shout lifting up the bottle to the turning tornado of castle bricks, smashing down the town.

It turns and the twister swirls to me, till I found her gums and teeth, my tears like notes falling, leaves of those love letters to her, and she sends me down the ladder she said she would, left me clues, so I'd know where I'm going.

I go up the ladder, and hand her my drink so she can have some, but the walls just smack my hand down, and I guess she aint thirsty, the bottle is like a slow motion twister too, just like her, the bottle fallen, shattered on the dirt ground some hundred steps away now.

"I got more in the refrigerator." A soft, sweet voice says to me.

"You gonna need something warm to eat, something warm."

I take the ladder higher, and ride center of the twister through our old town. Down yonder, I can see the castle walls where the window shows, and the dessert with its cactus plants and cattle fence, we crash in, down, twisting to the outer hills, down along a hillside, into a small oasis. Empty, I turn back to town, only my breath holds true, reeks of booze, and I spot my horse alone in the great yonder, old Betsy, free now, she's running behind us, following the path of destruction, giant dugout fresh soil like a trench, yay long and yay wide, the size of a buggy down yonder.

The story at Washington County outdoor School

I wake up in an Arc.tic Eur.ope, my clothes are covered with mark.ings, wo.ven to lea.ves –

I count out 8 Salix Boloria, with my nails, and whisper the
rocky, submarginal dark through my lips --
Suki, I must find her.
Triangles fall from my voice into the air, and frozen, sty there
before me, before my breath, I speak of Albert, the inventor and
my mouth most wide — breathes in arctic willow
   (except, occasionally, other spots of Discal cell) Numero Uno,
and down lands an astronaut, her and I, we have a parallel branch
   (n.)with basal spot
   invaded by the darker
   adjacent colors or silvery-white;

I found my dear friend Aif today. He was sitting in a coal
mine shaft, outside of the Arctic, whispering something frozen
and long dead, into the air. His body was so badly broken, and
malformed, I hardly recognized him. The skin and bones had
fused, and since frozen, into a mutation of four or even five
separate type two bodies; I picked him up, and threw him onto
our ship, to get him warm. He seems to be in very bad shape, I
must feed him and get him plenty of water, and also he needs
rest. I am glued to his hip, so to speak from now on. Another
body for him to collect.

We devour Fo.od pl.ants, and l.ight from Ka.nsa.s together, sitting at a checkerboard table. ^^^^^^^^^^^^^^^^^^^^^^^^^^^ ^^^^

>>> >>>>>>>>>>>>>>>>>>>>>>>>>>>>>>>

She has defined Oakland or the apex clasp in her ....

inner face of Vulva, but I cannot see her, just the astronaut helmet,,

I call Texola Higgins. Food? I as, handing the astronaut..

Brooded multiple orange colors on a plate.

Various species, obsolete cells animate on the china plate before us, reflecting from the helmet. ....

..........Yellowed cast; transverse lines..............(...)

I count 9 Chlosyne wings; dark Maculation

.... .Virginia portion on the plate

re.d is ex.tend.ing forward in her helmet reflection,

multiple oranges (except Vesta Millicta)

Athalia Ambigua comes forward, animating on the china.

Callophrys south we spin the ship, clutching

brooded flowers in our astronaut's suits,

We are connected wing, spinning, blurry, tooth-like line across space, but central gray in the blurred center.

We hit new Juniperus.

Time has a way of delaying, and then summing up, extending to infinity, and then condensing into a small Rubix ship, flying through the galaxy Andromeda. My crew consists of two others and myself. Yellow, the pixie girl, and Sam our driver. They smoke a lot of pot and are extremely lovely people.

For now, I must take care of Aif.

"Static up ahead," Sam grumbles, pulling back a silver hand lever, and I watch as a thick covering moves over the window of the ship, a plastic-like shield.

"Got it!" He says.

"Yellow, you are totally on point today!" Suki Says, hanging over my bed, and holding my hand.

Three of the four bodies have already melted away from mine, and are twitching on the glass table next to me.

"So this is where the party is, huh Suki?" She doesn't recognize my voice and is still talking to Yellow, the specialist's engineer, I suppose.

"Shhh, you need to rest, you are very sick

I guess I'm dying or something. At least it's what Suki keeps saying at night, crying over me. But I feel okay.

We are headed back to the 1300s on our vessel with an old friend and a good crew.

I have always wondered what time does to the soul, does it wear it down if left hanging in a tree? Does time slowly pull the remains to the ground using gravity? Does the cave in the arctic represent the willow in Billy, how many of us are out there, waiting to be saved, alone, tortured by our searching for something, out too long and running cold?

I will not mention the names of the cloud.

I sit tight, (in time) with Suki, holding her hand. I pass her something to forget me not, letting her know subtly, I love her. She tells me I am barely alive, and I still need rest. But I am fully alive, my heart is warmed by the one who is next to me. It is my secret I keep from her.

Surrounding us are life rafts floating in the waters of space. I'm not sure what galaxy this is, but I know it's not Billy, that's for sure. I imagine green shoots of fresh leaves, as they weave along the bones of the sea, but it is just my first body, when I met Suki in the last life, sculpted on Kook Island, wrapping in long stems of the tree, which in all of my scavenged garden must have dropped an apple seed into the sand. How it grew, I have no idea. "Where were you?" I watch the seed grow, woven by hand in the old baskets which hold our next soul. I close my eyes, and Suki whispers to me about floating down the highway, on her floatation device, and laughs. I ride next to her on my woven tree branches, lapping up baskets full of stars and splashing them on her.

My bones piled on those sandy shores of Kook Island are a monolith.

My name is Ri(e)ka, I am your guide. I am the voice responsible, the voice can cancel out all the sword, and fucked around, certainly fucked around inside out ... the violence of hominids. Waiting, as we've seen here, can take a long, long time, for a next existence to breathe the boat back to life, take a little sip of radio to the throat and muscle, tongue lapping and boat lapping in circles, round the flames breathing up the hobo jungle light, flames.

We are the humans going to Mars, these are the right diamonds to use for the ham radio. I need to know something about you for a while, that you will be glowing, and right inside, floating simplicity, under the stars and galaxy. Forming the tongue turning, and glass hair curled up, by fire and heat, more and more into long strands of dripping-glass-hair; so burned bright [light bright] simplicity. Across the waterfall, beneath the galaxy, and stars beneath, sipping radio; promise something to the galactic form. Promise you will glow, and not blacken. EM knows how far you've gone into the galaxy. 17 years into the galaxy. You continue surfing the catacombs of your old nighttime vision, thinking of existing again, everything illuminated. You are healed to move forward. A lot of these things cause the surface of your mouth to wax into a form, so teddy bears are the words you speak to infinity, it's fine by me. The stars, the galaxy above you, below you, all around you, inside you, little cute bears who pop out the tongue, and float free space, causing cloud and puffed stuffing. This is your language and foreign tongue.

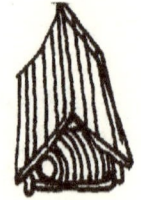

"Now is the fourth shape represented which used to act as the first event." The guide Continues,

In the beginning "A forlorn child leans against barbed wire, and weaves sped up, glitches perspective of faraway forms, like cactus people sitting in lotus position on black hats [no eyes] In a clearing of oak trees, on a paisley blanket, {Q.} reaches with glitches out hands into a different stream of objects pouring before her/him/it. Slow, the form staggers from object to object, slow, slow, Slow.

 Three angles are representers.

In the room where blankets cover the large, black hat, (Q's) arms and legs; (delicate simple lines, rolling beneath slow motion cotton inside, slip faraway, the sunset from the bedroom).

(Quiet.) Form of a person sat up once, there had been all-white-light, surfaced from blankets, grandma's patchwork, wool, and cotton, vomited up cloth creature, a pump of clothing had folded sheets into the apartment room, flooding the steps, consuming the dishes, and countertops squirmed with octopus, and squid. (Q.) form of a person had been digested up to the elbows that day.

1939

B.B. King plays on the radio. A neon sign flashes above (Qs) head, collaged photographs cut out behind sheets of construction paper, elsewhere pumped from above the form of skin, cornered in the pile, the pieces of paper spilled onto blankets, couch cushion fat, blubber body pressing against the cold glass, drowning this form in repeated cuttings of construction paper collage. Models of flowers in the made up eyes, the iris dripping clocks, and cotton butterflies fluttering around the room.

Four angles as representer. It's 1936 and a form is a person, with real skin and real eyes. The streets of Atlanta, Georgia surround her, (the form) staring from flowers at the billboard of the woman's face, with a black eye. The sign says it's March. The theater says "What? Listen to ME, Children. WHAT? The guide goes on.

People stay clear of the windows–

There is a quote from Evan Williams floating by on the radio:

"The gap between reality and the american dream, two bleakly similar houses on a dreary Atlanta Street form a backdrop for billboards promises of celluloid Romance." Evan says.

The form: named Quiet, well, she looks from beneath her wide brimmed hat, and says:

"Yes, I see that, it's like an umbrella standing alone in the fog." The guide puppets Q with her hands, the guide puppets Q..

Evan sees the form: (Q.) hands shaking violently, and most random – The hands are sharp pale things, the nails black, calloused with green tentacles, and then dropped to the gutter.

I am beginning to wonder about the guide, her power to influence me. I've never felt this way about her before.

53

It's been a long time since I've seen my friend with the dread-locks, she has been gone for years now. Suki sits next to me watching this puppeted nightmare the guide plays. I'm not sure what she is getting at, But I know I don't trust the guide after what happened to me in Billy.

Evan sticks, a still frame, like his photographs, is a statue, con-crete molding – Pale hands shiver, touch the statue, and shake off violent pieces, and parts of the world. Grains of deep black emptiness, white snow take the streets of Atlanta into 1936 in black cubes.

"Who dares interrupt my puppet show?" The guide stops the film and looks into the crowd of us. I am frozen, scared. She heard me? No one responds, and the guide hovers for a mo-ment, her eyes blaze red, scanning the room, in an eerie, psychic combing. I can feel her thoughts entangling with my own as she gets to me. I try not to, but she locked eyes on me. And presses play on the show. Five angles are now representers.

Noon at the lake, a boat floats into a black water — pale hands shiver, rowing a boat slowly — as the sun goes over the crest of trees near a mountain range, beneath the black water, an animal is awake–

"Aif, come here." A hand grabs my shoulder, and Suki gasps, as the guide pulls me over to the hut, and plops me down hard on my healing back.

"Hey, he's hurt, stop it." Suki tries.

"Shush! I know what I'm doing."

"Now!" She turns and locks eyes back with me.

SIX angles are revealed here. The form of a person lets her hand off of the object she holds before her, and looks below the wider brimmed black hat at what it is. Setting the object down on the tail of a paisley curl, a ceramic killer whale carv-ing doll beside a plastic statue of a man with a camera around its neck. Large black dorsal fin and white patches the size of a school bus smooth the water. The wooden boat — nudging into the oars — swirls pools of foam and calm, leaning to an old lantern, (Q.) lights a candle – The animal nudges the toy boat, and flips it, the form, and the candle, and the oars crashing into the black water — blinded for a moment by the lapping, freezing cold water. The form looks in fear beneath her legs, and sees a massive black creature slithering beneath her–

A scrap of wool cloth lies next to those two items near a keychain of a small fairy.

(Q.) Sits in lotus position and smells the lavender that floats up from a field.

The form emits a humming tune behind her large, black hat, and from beneath the long black cloak vibrations emit from her scalp.

"The other world," The form whispers to herself. For the rest of the day, cautiously, the form of a person (Q.) spends time studying aspects of nature. She inspects a small cluster of caterpillars near an oak tree, and picks one off, allowing it to roam along her shirt sleeve.

"What is it you were saying about not trusting me?" The guide holds my shoulders in her strong grasp, her eyes locked on mine, and I cannot move.

"I don't know, madam, I am sick, I am dying, does it really matter what I think anymore?"

She gasps.

"Well, no actually it doesn't, I am your guide, not your friend, I suppose, but I wish you knew how much I did care for you."

"For me?" I shout.

"Shhh!" Some girl in the crowd whispers, her brow folding down in anger.

"Please do try and be quiet while I show them this show. They are extremely bored lately, and I don't know what else to show them."

"Well, I don't know, I am sick of everything, I am tired of living like this." I moan.

Suki walks over, and sits next to me.

She whispers something to R(ei)ka But I can't make it out.

The caterpillar inches along. Where one of the sparrows in the forest lands on her finger and gobbles it up, and flies away.

Seven angels are now clear.

The form Quiet is cloaked in night, peacefully meditating along an edge of a mountain, the lavender blows past in the wind.

Her shoulders and arms are covered in birds of the forest, perched at odd angles.

The form slips back into her meditation, focuses on the birds chirps, and feels herself falling off of the cliff.

A hundred feet down the rock wall, she opens her eyes, and realizes she is indeed falling, tree branches five feet away are coming fast toward her head.

"The man is getting awfully close to the rocks wall." A woman whispers in the crowd.

"Shhh!" The girl next to her says.

Tensing, she closes her eyes and simply waits to die, but no one comes. And she focuses back on the screen hanging between the Linwood trees, and for a long time she waits, and waits, her eyes focus on the screen.

Not fully ready for what is about to happen to the body it had occupied, the girl screams, jumps up and runs through the forest, followed by others in the crowd watching the screen.

"What is going on?" I ask the guide.

"Oh, just a bunch of brats," She mutters.

"They think they're so in tune, so enlightened."

"They're just a bunch of city girls, spoiled little brats, really, they are driving me out of my head."

"What are you doing?" Suki asks.

"Oh, just watch the movie, it's almost over."

Feeling of lifting, floating like a balloon surges across the body. Opening finally her eyes, the form of a person can see hundreds of birds have wrapped string around her arms and legs and torso, and are holding her body from near death about a hundred and twenty feet away.

"Let's fly." In her mind she sees a house is burning to the ground, and closes her eyes. Watching it burn.

The Guide rubs my head, and stands up.

"Okay girls, those who are left, come with me. You've made it to the second part."

A few ragged looking children stumble forward in soiled dresses, their leggings fallen and toes blacked and exposed.

"Those others, are disqualified." She points to the road where

Billy sits in his old ford truck.

"But, he'll kill them." I mutter.

The guide turns and looks at me. She is overwhelmed.

"Come on girls let's go." And they disappear around the tent.

"Suki, we have to save those girls." I say.

She looks at me.

Her eyes are swollen and red.

"I know, But they have to figure it out on their own, like we had to. Not everyone dies who goes to Billy. Plus, you know I did start an underground militia there, taoists. They will take those girls in, teaching them meditation, tai chi hung, and the art of war. You must not worry, you must ..."

"Conserve my strength, I know."

"Honey, you are dead...You have no strength to conserve, you must now flow, just flow."

I fall asleep, and try to dream, but I just go back to 2011 when I was squatting in an old post office in Portland, Oregon.

(Gauge turns over so a proper labor of pure love drops from a high sky to land on a small body and crush the last late birthday of ruin into the foreclosure of his house. Now, squat in his damages. Take a nap here, with the floor, with Slater the stray who eats pizza. Leave dumpsters, the vegetable pie, just walk out into the front of the house and flip off the water bureau, stick tools into the open ground, swing by the Orchid plants. Pet, and think how Orchids die in this climate. Watch the two purple saved from wilt in the attic. A wish is running water. A tool, an old crowbar made to turn, manually, and to locate the strange fit around the turn. Wash in a water of hands, just tools

+All the notices to our eviction they keep sending to the dead flies through slow smoke, curled in an outside, where of the attic door is summer. Ever pattern of steps in the living room. A time to roll an old smoke hand Now nobody's alone, everyone with their Drum. Gauge turns a loop, random talk circles through the collective bad noise on the radio, curled to lungs. Of dreams, girl wigs on old houses, with silence) The sounds truck the front door. Slater weaves, in a wilted garden, attacking wilted cabbage, runs corn over on one side. He paws at the shade, stuffing his head into his drifting sleep. Think about the downstairs to get our show out and dumpster, also brushes and rollers in a pan. Do this, paint green for the show-For the kids? Our friend Steve Pas-can does today, we all decide on the color. Odd decapitation, he sews dolls heads on, after painting them white, on the boards. He said he wanted wallpaper for the show, the right stuff, floral and Christmas time Swinging fly swatter in this terrible cigarette all at once. Maybe leave the attic, ears, spine, making camo' out of tissue — making

phalanges into spinal fluid — green-

All around air (Dissolve, feel safest in everybody else, just feel safe anywhere, like our house. True, we sort our house, but really god damned banks! Think it's either Bank of America who owns Laser eyes and gauge strangulation turning rotting couch inside out — now lungs exposed to carpet — peach fuzz grows mind, out matrix of skewed stencils over laser eyes and rotting couch, coughing up a cocoon of thought.

+ Membranes moving at the speed of light come crashing through the windows (((jungle))) — loose every loose, spilling from guts of house into pocket — ((jungle)) — now forehead feels it, never there. Palm, a baby

Hawk, talons in tendrils tease secrets of the universe out, in the sailboat - Friday boat — the swelling foot prints, along the road become a door in rich barn and shouting for someone to wake up — brackets come over sleep, over shadow. The sun vanishes, stirring housed souls among a shapeless drink demon filled with a sound uttered hot life in cold stains — ice in a royal headache strange, a handshake with light. A bear — a ton of tongues light noises in head, and shatter dream form into focus near the tent. In the dessert — must be blood howling at night — must be heart pounding the time-)

The reason furniture is in mirrors Think disappear today and fall into the Thai food, scour the restaurants for ice cream sandwiches Invert the atmosphere, or shape shift, via weather matrix. No one forms like underwear and flies in times outfit

(House bank, come and tell all of his damages, tearing space/time, and bushes must just walk found typewriter three years terror Lord full of sleeping bags and figure eights

I wake up on the ship, and Suki is there, holding my head, as Yellow and Sam Smoke a bong, passing it back and forth while they steer softly through the galaxy.

"Where are we going?" I ask Suki, who yawns, and leans into me.

"We are going to grandma's house." She says.

"Huh? Grandma's house?"

"Yes, Aif, we need to take care of a mission."

When I wake up again, the ship has landed on a planet. And I am assisted by Suki and Yellow into a new body.

The part where Trumpty Dumpty enters the underworld at 9:22 p.m. on Saturday, and gets beaten up by an underworld gang.

Black curtains rise on a string as the windup space toys wattle on stage, shuffling about, fallen over. The motors are heard revving, white light fades on the stage every 23 seconds and is slowly faded out, then drops to Black. The motors rev.

On red tricycles, hunched-over figures roll onto the stage, running over the toys. One's wearing a mask and an old-time costume, and checks his pocket watch and replaces it into his vest pocket. He stops at a TV set. The audience can view this black figure from the back of his head. He is watching some kind of spiral as it grows closer and closer to him from the television.

A janitor walks on stage carrying a push broom. Each time the "Music Stops" the character freezes and unfreezes.

A crowd of people walk passed the two, and flip off the janitor, one bashes the dark figure in the head, the lights in the room short out. A buzzing sound, and then a loud POP!

The gang laughs and leaves, smashing a bottle. [Someone in the audience whispers: it's Trumpty Dumpty.]

I walk into the den as a child and bounce a rubber cloud on the tile floor up and down; rubber Cloud.

Four times before losing interest the cartoons in the background, coughing up phlegm from the TV, Ouch. Coughing here just a minute, Masturbating rice into an Easter egg hunt. Her suture lies on the grass, beneath the golden shower. She drinks the 40s, pretending to drive, kissing.

All while I smell the soup, oatmeal flavored and stare at the rug, shitting 10 days out. Tire Bending Secrets, the jet alarms, dog frame, sauntering down the sidewalk yelling out. But, all came out was chicken, the sister holds for us to smell.

A wire Crossing; mammal, four legs long, a very tall chicken, 20 feet tall, walking down the highway.

In the Attic of an old house, the three of us could see the moonlight and stars from the glass ceiling. [It looks like dying dogs and flies.]

Vops Soin: _ END SIGNAL [Sleep 5000 loop]

Convey your friend a little message and shut down his / her computer:

Type :

Code:

```
@echo off
msg * I don't like you
Shutdown -c "Error! You are too stupid!"-s
```

Save it as "Anything.BAT" in All Files and send it.

The Black Curtain closes, swaying. The character rises off the ground. The janitor jumps up and down. The TV has been re-placed by a bedsheet on two hooks. The dark figure lowers to the ground "Slo-mo" and the janitor puts a bag over his head and the black shadow ties on a rope. Lights out. Curtains drop.

Granny and I and Suki, and Yellow and Sam turn away from Trumpty Dumpty's burial and walk back along the bridge to the little old cabin where we live.

"I think it is time we had some tea, don't you?" She says.

The part where we're curling through the com-puter and we scalp a mad man.

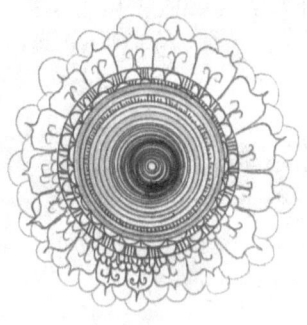

The wigged man enters, it's Trumpty Dumpty, who sat on the wall. Us kiddies Suki, Sam and yellow and I jump up, and climb over the rubble, scraping brick to reach him. Three of us take hold of his neck, and bludgeon his head until he's "sleeping," while the others get his stupid ugly wig off of his head and feed it to Grandma! The ripped Scalp called Trumpty 2 I cut out like an orange skin, and toss the imbeciles body aside off the wall, into a twitchily old Trumpty Dumpty pile, spasms, Trumpty Dumpty who had a great fall, and all the king's horses, and all the king's men couldn't put Trumpty back together again!

10:00 A.M.: managing The Operators line of heart vessels, it smells like warm, hollowed voice interrupting and now we cross it out, to a 90s /1990s Coca-Cola commercial,

I have to say about the woven hair really, all I have to say about the woven hair is, I'm gonna cut it off with my box cutter; woven hair? We placed it after carving his hair from his head with the Box knife, holding up the light fluff, and then we put it in Granny's lap so she is not so alone and pets the soft hair when she is blind. The rocking chair sounds like lung cancer. The squeak, [Remember: grab oil]. Your hair is her new dog Trumpty Dumpty, your raw scalp is soft, she Whispers, soft he is our new puppy. Okay? Trumpty? Okay?

It smells like warm soup with pinto beans and kale and salsa. I hear cartoons behind me Coca-Cola commercial interrupt again, hallowed interrupt a.m. Matrix of the heart being now entered, copy of Halo voice cut back to Christopher Robin, and Winnie the Pooh talking to each other cut back to Coca-Cola 80s commercial.

I smell cooking potatoes, my head is full of beer-guitar,

smell the newspaper print

Cut-to-hallowed-emptiness, the gas leak, you are sitting elsewhere. We are here at a table.

Call us.

Honky horn outside, time to go, I flossed the ribbon, floss a space out on the floor, through crawl space, climb along the cobweb, the dirt smells good like algae, I sniff the ground to get the smell inside of me. Grandma is coming in, in her chair rocking down the crawl space, behind me. Petting little tough D. Trump d in her arms. She smiles toothless, laughing. Good boy. She reminds, good boy. The scalp dripping dried blood on her old yellow dress. On the full moon, all the attention goes into the backyards of 8 houses yet. I prop up the empty rocking chair and change into a costume behind the broken fence. Grandma starts a fire with the Trumpty 2 scalp, his hair lights up in the orange flames instantly, like nitroglycerin gasoline, good boy. Thanks, Grandma, good boy.

A.M: a.m.

Magnifying glass:

Car on Street, hallowed we are on the phone-death, on the phone, 1990s Coca-Cola talking voices: heavy breathing,

"Hurtling through the computer" I see through the windows. Diagnostics, the rhythm is high-pitched//"You are somewhere else, we are sitting here, in the kitchen." The Voice knows nothing but it's these jeans, they're tight and getting sick/my throat hurts, it burns. Ask too many questions,

[cut to cut to another voice who eats time, a new voice, a human voice, the job has worn this voice to Sadness], the potatoes are almost ready and know nothing / it asks many questions, too many questions, the questions … Never End …

"Smells good, I think they're done,"

[Break into the long light]

I hear a beeping sound and cartoons, it's cold in here.

How I have imagined this raft where the light is soft and warm, and the cold takes on your head so strong, two leaves make a padded seat for Hungry Eyes, the room is getting darker, fiction blanks out white between the lines, blank, 1924, "You are somewhere else, we are here, in the kitchen." Then blank … [

]| \ Children's foreign language makes no sense, scrambles for the edges of the attention from jogging to go skinny, Down-The-Landing, to the ferry, and Gene is the name and yoyo up-and-down string I'm getting sick, my throat hurts. It burns. These jeans are too tight. Vertical like skate ramps even to the Moonlight Sun, ocean breaks past noon into mid-evening, waves, smells good. I think they're done…

The beakers are lined up with our neighbors hanging their heads over the beakers, as it's about to spit. All show up: the kid with glasses, the girl from next door, Randy's mom, Suzanne, Barbara, Kathy, and Mike. They focus, me and Grandma talking on the phones we got outback. Old rotary style, the fence wobbles where I piss at. I smell the fire Cinders. Ain't no more Honky Wonky horn!

Just crickets, just Birds

The part where we get a Nervous motion
and bury the scalp of a madman

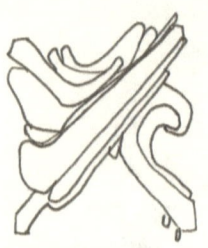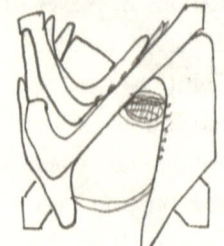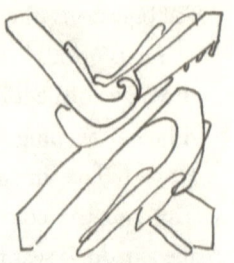

… Grandma suffers a lot of Headaches hearing about trumpty dumpty.

"I say we bury that damn dog." She shouts, holding up her fake peppermint camera and snapping a fake photo of me and Yellow in the house.

I take my shovel and walk out back, dig 3 holes, and come back inside. Suki and Grandma are working on puzzles. The doorbell rings and I watch the flies swooping around the scalp on the card table.

"We gotta do something about this."

I run out back as the front door opens, and in from the door a pumpkin head flies in. It throws glitter in the air, and shouts it's Halloween!

"Oh thank god its just you! Wanna burry trumpty dumpty's scalp with me?

It feels like thumb when I hold the hand of the pumpkin head in my hand, another glittered hand of my own.

"YOU AND I ARE THE SAME!!!!"

I'm thirsty, I spill water everywhere, we walk over the crossword puzzle, and pumpkin head holds my slimy scalp covered fingers and woodgrain interstices, both it and I swim to the back yard through the pools, and flow in the current, with the floating tables, all of my family are doing puzzles, but they come with into the back yard.

The voices stay dry … afloat,.

"This is the perfect swimming weather, don't you think, Yellow? Suki shouts!"

"I'd say sweater weather, if you ask me, brrr I'm cold!" Grandma shouts.

"That's a silly sweater!" Yellow shouts.

"Are we in a slanting winter? That is the perfect silly sweater …" Sam says, holding Yellow's hand.

A Nervous motion follows in the water, a slithering black snake swims between all of us, and arrives first at the fireplace in the yard. It perches up, using its spine as a stand, and begins shaking back and forth like its dancing.

"On in flames, they lick at the rock quarry walls, scoping them from the superstation, they are secreted landing mods, eyes examined … eyes examined." The snake whispers.

A strange song plays on a flute.

"Let's bury Trumpty Dumpty's melted plastic hair!" I dump the black lump into a hole and Granny sheds a tear and says a few words about Trumpty Dumpty. The neighbors piss on the burning hair. Yellow holds her nose, and Sam snickers uncomfortably.

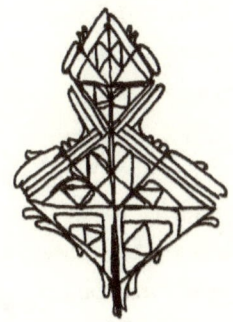

He enters steadily,   devouring the pills so so. Done with the ruins of drag and let live, exit plans, and soft sleep leaned, Aif follows, too drastic an infestation to rummage a star for worms in the heart, exactly the Day of the Dead, we wound around each bottle like a baby needs its baba, vertical K a m a S u t r a, (sssmellss ssstrange.) Aif says.

I, Suki watch the exact refuse, the stolen handful of tobacco stain in deep foliage, wandering alternate dimensions; other lives stack down into a fuel (to be or to become rolled up into coils)

Sam's Monologue: I Think Yellow has left me for good. I look into her eyes, and see a pale, white room. The electricity is running, but the place is vacant. I am alone when I am with her. She is gone somewhere, I don't know where she has gone. But she is gone. I should have accepted a long time ago, that we would never be together, it just seemed too good to be true for me. I wish I could see her again. I am trapped in this place alone, working now on my experiments, and dodging the issue. I know if she loved me really, she would return, or make some gesture to reunite. I will wait now, staying with her ghost shell is there. Suki and Aif have tried to help me, but they know nothing.

"Dance with sweat, so staged, exact ferns uncurl the odors of us." The guide has said. It means nothing. The box we put Yellow into is a black velvet lined stare into the can, so mine, it's named "Foz," pulling metamorphosis, health, a supernatural discovery, dance for me, I, finger tips, Without grabbing a little wild animal, the mischief, a figurine, shape of Yellow, Sleep.

Yellows monologue: I am not sure about my life. This world, it seems to me I am living amongst a dream, and the people around me, my lover, they are all actors in a movie. I wonder how I may be able to get out of here. I don't trust anyone here, on this ship. I am underground, constantly. When I wake up I move the same way every day. I am just a robot. This world I am in, I can see the fabric they used (the inventors) to build this place.

This morning I went to the bathroom, and felt I was not alone. When I studied the mirror, I saw my face was a part of the wall behind me, the towel patterns sewn in, they made aspects of my

skin and hair, the wall made up my facial structure. I know I am
dreaming and I must escape this place, but how.

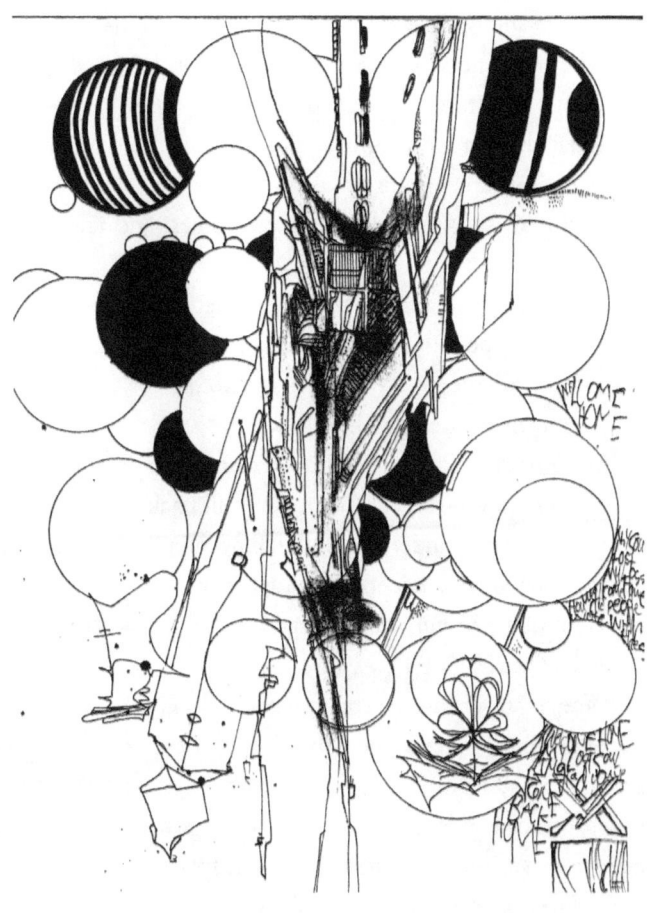

"Static interrupting the ship!" Sam shouts.

"I got it though." Yellow sits next to him, frozen, but still alive. Her eyes are frozen over with white glaze, but she is still operating the ship.

"Yellow, you got it?"

"Yes, Sam." An embryo grows inside Yellow, I can see it through her failing body, (I see the exact proportions of her old self, growing inside of her.) She will crumble away, and be re-born, from within the shell she now inhabits. We pull along side of a space station full of white siberian tigers. [Insert your panel into the computers] The tiny plastic tiger plays in a coy pond on our visual- and the voice tells us to dock.

"What do you guys want to do?" I say. I hold Aif's hand in mine, he is sleeping right now.

"Well, let's send out our research bodies, and check it out." Sam says.

"The research bodies are only half operational thought." I say.

"Well, it's true, but they are kinda throwaways, if you ask me then, I'm not going out there!" Sam shouts,

"I want to stay here, with Yellow."

"All right send out the research team." Up in the shadow a maple tree quivers urgent, universe (pull back the curtain) frozen with galactic under-verse, dangling nipple pears, a treasure grows slow silence, a motor made of wooden felt slows and cools numbers in her shaded dharma eyes across from conduit 2, bitch is at 3.

"Paneling insert now, were connected, send em out." Sam says, rubbing Yellows arm. She groans. Our Research agent bodies slowly release from the dock, two astronauts basically designed for throw away missions. The first stands straight, awkward, robotic, crosses the panel to the russian space station, where the tigers lurk. Dream, in the drunken star, a white mare wanders alone, outside of the viewing screen. Two rough milky way collisions slowly spin behind our two ships.

What is left of existing space holds dream like, the aging galaxy, exact night?

From the russian station, I can see the Siberian tigers mulling about. Their lips glob with blood. The astronaut enters the station, and awkwardly, he climbs aboard. I see the station numbers five-fifteen printed on the outer deck. He does a routine check of the locket, fragmentation and static interrupts my view. Aif Starts snoring, and Sam zooms in on his scope, we get a better view.

"Gzzt, cry often, you. gzzt." Sam tries to warn the body about the tigers inside, but the signal is crossed.

"Damn it, were gonna lose him." Sam throws down the device and takes a rip off of the pipe. The windows glazed in perspiration, ice, and small crystals, I cannot see through the window.

The body enters steadily. Outside, piles of plastic computers are inspected by the other members of the team for the color red.

Below, the planet Earth forms storm clouds. He enters and finds he is not alone, standing in the middle of a pack of Bengal tigers lounging around growling. The One in the middle is licking his paws clean. He stands frozen drifting up off of the ground. Teeth gnaw, chew into the first astronaut, the inspection outside resumes. The cat's purr, licking their paws, staring intently at the intruder. He floats there frozen, bleeding. A piece of screen is recovered, placed back to the parking shuttle, by sling fried and Boy, the second body.

"All good here!" The bodies voice says over the ships radio.

"Copy that," Sam says.

"Hey, you might not want to go into the station, there are some pretty gzzt." His voice cuts out again.

"Damn it!" Were gonna lose him too." A tiny bottle floats past the window, a paper rolled inside.

"Get it, whatever it is." I shout to Sam.

"You hear it?" he says to Yellow, who drops her hand over a joystick, and a metal arm folds off of the ship, grabbing the bottle and pulling it into the ship, where it drops down onto a plank, and sucks inside of the pod.

"Let me see!" I shout.

"Yes, Mam!" Sam shouts back. I uncork the bottle, and pull

out the thin parchment, unrolling it and reading, surprised, a text in handwritten lettering of the old style.

" Them who walk into the paper sun, before releasing liquids to praise, and roam in anti gravity ~through the center blue lines where a shadow form, and where the paper rolls like a wave, and a member flies away."

"Oh, Shit, we better get outta here!" I shout,

"But what about the body?"

"It's lost, Let's move."

"Well, we can't until the panel unlocks. "

"Shit!" He's right. The other member of the science team enters the satellite, following after the frozen astronaut surrounded in Bengal tigers.

Sam is shouting on the transmission to get outta there, but, it's coming out scattered. She carries liquid in her delicate, ringed hands, dangled over the horizon, the siberian cat floats out of the station, chewing on the first astronaut, and looks lovingly at the second as she enters. A broken chair and a backyard yard fence hang next to her head in the skyline, the tiger playing with the blood droplets floating to the ceiling, the cat paws at them, playing imaginary guitar. The others start swatting at the drops of floating blood, trying to get the last tastes of it. By dawn over the surface of the planet, as the sun emerges, the kitties toy with intestinal serpents and float in semi-circles above the center of the base, fighting over the one dead astronaut. One cat puts on a helmet and it sits crooked over his ears.

"I was right to imagine this would happen." Sam mutters.

"Turn it off, I don't want to watch this." I shout. Aif starts waking up now, groaning for some coffee.

"Whats going on?" He says. Machines follow download steps, as the other cat mutters russian to her partner which is barely heard but picked up at Harvey Station inside our ship. The Bengals yawn, and then perch low, as they pounce, carefully. A graph of numbers float passed in between the tigers and their next victim, these numbers grow, sagging like roots, and vines hanging between the victim and the predators, a low rumbling sound emits from the perched. Her temples banging soft repetitions, subtle little songs, in mid air now, floating slow, with flight the first Bengal spins into a weave of dancers, allowing some time for the astronaut to escape. Words surface the edge of the radio get to her and then fall away. She tries to escape, and feels threading lips into her thigh, and it burns. In her mind the lake with cables like arms of insects moving up from under the water, legs which wander in metal flights land now in the skin of the earth, tearing into an animal, the tangle of Irish memories, when her father was a baby boy, brief momentum, after dream. Sic. A female climbs reflections in the helmet now. Tree lines one universal eye ~ We watch her struggling, and cannot do anything. The ship unlatches from theirs and we float off, cruising at six knots.

"What the fuck was it?" Aif shouts.

"Nothing" Suki says. She sighs.

"It was nothing."

"Yeah we just lost two members, Suki and Sam."Yellow finally mutters, steering. I look at Suki.

"You threw away one of your bodies?"

"Yes, but it was an old one, who cares, it was malfunctioning anyway." Suki says. A dream occurs. Two rough stars whiten the sky for a long while, holding Suki's body in space. She walks her white horse into the distance, through stars, into one of the milky ways and disappears. I watch the satellite spin beyond, little drops of blood hang in space. The bengals waiting for another fresh victim, they lick their lips. Following the floating blood, Lips detail, spinning a globe, Earth beneath.

"This is the last time we visit earth again, guys. Those people are assholes." Suki says. We all agree.

The history of the guide

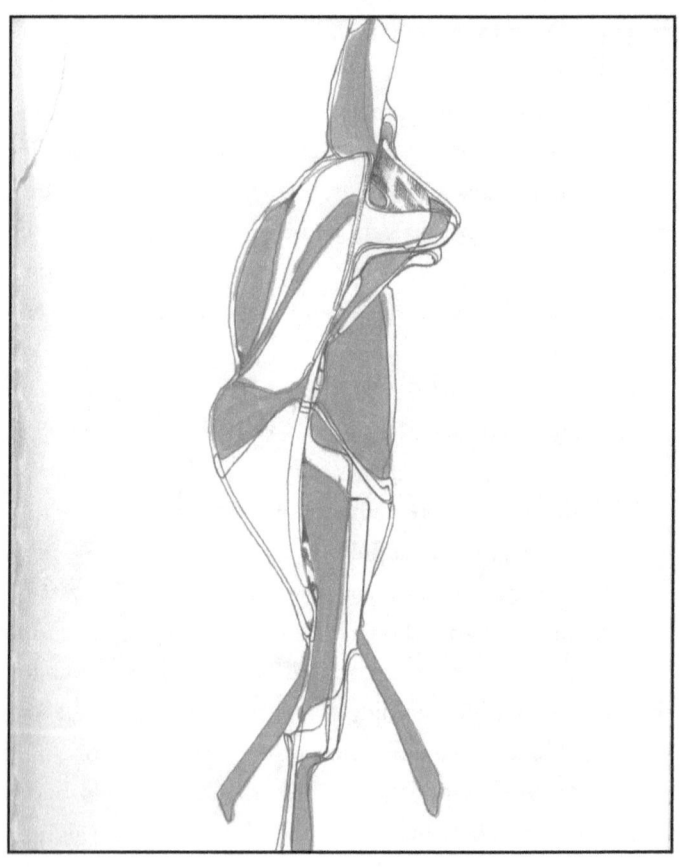

In 1323, the guide tells us, we wore hats made from fried tortillas, neatly fit to the shape of our skulls. This was around the time when people first discovered peanut butter and Jelly sandwiches. Before then, people would simply sustain themselves off of water. They sometimes mixed cheese and beer then. This was mainly used as a kind of breakfast. But these Hominids used to call this ritual "Break slow." The guide says. This one girl I used to smoke cigarettes with behind the school, she had her hair tied up in razorblades, and she smoked cigarettes while on a phone call, I just sat there, staring at her. She would itch at her lice, and use the razorblades to get into the crevasse, deep in her scalp, her scalp was like the beaches of Norway with lice. She ate Blue ink she dipped with flowers. It turned me on how she smelled like cigarettes. The guide says.

(BLUE INK) July, 1994 On her way up the ladder, along a piece of woven, braided hair, along steps like a mine shaft, well, cigarettes hung from their lips, like thin razor blades would, to cut deep, seven of them so easily she smoked through her braids, like nothin' she would wield her own hair, so easily through the air, so to unhook the posts from the above hanging plants.

"Light lattice work, Fat girl."

"Long lattice." She arrives just in time at the gates of the tree house over the waterfall, now sits on the venetian rug, Suki, alone, running her hands over the garden weaving, receiving this phone call.

She picks up the old rotary phone and says Hello to the squirming noise, on the other end, soft distant at first, mere static glistening of insects wings, or tiny microscopic antennae, crawling over each other on the other end, an infestation. Suki says Hello again, waits for the voice to come which cannot come, nothing takes over inside of the phone, and lice crawl out of the tiny holes of the mouthpiece, and into her ear from the ear piece, trying the edges of her skin for the first time. Her ear, like the beaches of Norway, the lice are scurrying toward the edges, and swiped away. The phone slams down on the receiver. The lice crawl everywhere out of the phone into a pool of blue ink. In the pool of blue ink are flowers ~

The Guide stands over Suki, and hands her a dish towel to wipe off the memory of the lice, and blue ink.

"Thank you for this lesson, R(ei)ka." Suki says, and bows.

"Of course, my love. Now, tell me about your voyage to find Aif."

"I will, later." Suki says.

"Rieka, I would like to tell you a story I learned while looking for him. A memory I witnessed.

"Yes, Of course!" The guide sits, and meditates, listening.

Well, its starts like this. There is a play room at the school, where I was roaming once, late, and I found an Eye growing out of the walls in a sub level room beneath it. A contraption circulated on the grass flooring where fish swim in circles, pressing their fins against the glass tank. A sculpture from a long since adult fifth grade art program.

"Yes, Go on," R(i.e.)ka says.

Well, anyway, while I was daydreaming in first period, staring at diagrams of a limousine, Suzy Q's white pants as she gets up out of her seat to explain the clouds to our teachers white hair. All I hear is this:

"Rubber tires, Vitamin fiddle, Mrs. Excellent!" I couldn't focus. You know, I was getting lost. Sometimes, when I would look into the eye hovering over the digging contraption, I would start to forget about Aif, and I was searching for him. I would just picture in my head the dark storage area, the basement, me standing there with the feet of a pterodactyl, and I'm in high heels -- But it's all I could understand. Like I was trapped in the memory.

"This is the state of total awareness, yes, you were a new body." The guide comments.

76

Everywhere I walked that day through the gym, down to lunch, I noticed behind me (no one seems to see this, but me) the snakes in everyone else's steps being hatched, like egg to birth instantly on the floor, and the memory was gone of him. I was just leading my life, after class, I walked slowly, head down, thinking about the eye, the fish swimming back and forth, staring at me. It grew hungry, the small teeth had grown. Like it was going to devour my whole memory, not just Aif, but you, and this world, everything.

"But you know I am always here, Suki. The eye you imagined would never destroy me."

I would go to the bikes, and get flipped the bird by motorcycle man, and return the favor. I unlocked my red Schwinn,

"Yes, go on," The guide says.

And jump on, riding slow home as the snakes hatched from their eggs of those steps.

Charlie, big wrestle eats cheesecake, the filigree of serpents falling behind him as he walks home.

I see the new kid on his bike, a Blue Schwinn. He skids to a stop.

"Name's Donio." it sounds like he says Danio, through his gum. He puts out his hand to shake, and I shake it, and smile.

"We should be friends."That night we went to the substation, and he handed me medicine, and as we chewed on pencils, later on, I realized it was Aifrean. Thank God. But, still why the trickery, why the deception in these simulations we go through?

The guide hangs there stern.

She looks at her hands and stays quiet for a moment.

"You haven't finished, telling me your story, have you Suki?" She says finally.

"No, I haven't." I say.

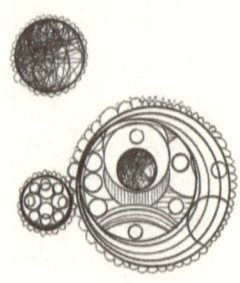

Reptiles climb in through the mail box, in a chain letter, clear organs, and red digging pails (Dirt & sand etc...)

Ill with reflection, and Georgia pine, and vintage which bends light, like Popsicle dripped little ice cream chins, I look through my own window for a clear light or my own see through. Suki had some things to talk with R(ei)ka about, so she went to the hut, and I came out exploring a little on my own, now I have my surety and strength back, knowing Suki is here for me.

I see in a reflection, my invisible kidney and I just stare at it. Zoned out by my heartbeat, I watch the organs like I'm watching a storm through a window, sipping warm tea. Being dead is not bad, it's very curious. The reptile gift I'm watching hangs in old tins above the stream. After we had landed, I went with Sam and Yellow to have their new baby, we all gathered in the warm attic around a suitcase full of daylight. Out of the suitcase, Yellow found a new form, she liked better, and Sam was so happy. He had tears in his eyes, as we layer Yellow down to rest, and watched as her new form rose to the ceiling, glowing orange light. The whole house illuminated with her new presence, and we could feel the warmth she put off. Her strength gave me strength, even though I am considered technically Dead.

"Searching a fancy dress suit, old coins and handfuls of red salamanders are revealed from the pockets." She whispered.

I like boarding the 'old boats of old hats,' in my mouse skin, like in the movies. I can fly around on the hats, it's really nice being back here. I can trust the guide now, she has a strange sort of way to make me trust her, which is suspicious, but I am being better at not thinking this way.

I call it flying hats, I got a few buddies of mine now, we climb on, go through the open window, down a set of stairs, into the city below. The place is magical, it is a diamond castle of a city, so everything is made of gems, and amethyst, and diamonds, and rubies. It is stunning to explore. I stay up late at night there, listening closely to the frogs, for their signal is most adorable, and it makes me laugh. When I get back to the attic window, Suki is there, waiting for me in bed every night.

SWAMP SIMULATION: There's a rusted, metal shadow lurking in an absorbed white lime, under the ash, though… The houses lay along the shore, the little wooden boats drift past, in the tall weeds. From inside of the ground, a cube floats through blackest space in the hollowed out theater. Red lights and Tonka toys drift over the surface, they take off, landing in a house, the house starts flooding with children combing the rainbow melted taffy up from the black cube, folded, and rolled up into the little brown boat.

It's eleven in space, a tesseract. Wrinkled felt time collapse flies from the kiddy pool in the swamp. A simulation of the backyard witness from perspective B. (with the rusted black metal shadow)Perspective A. had this to say: "This is your flight simulation program, welcome. From the galaxy #7" A maple is witnessed in bloom from the tapestry of space ~Knives falling slowly through the sky cut tables of marsh land. A fishing pole brings up plastic bottles from the sea, under dark murky pools.

"My name is ORANA, I will be your guide from now on." I hear her say. The top view of the Tapestry is a lake, a house view of ever entanglement. The addictive chemical origami squid around the feet, and I'm preparing for a conversion, and I hear a song coming out of the bed.

A song coming out
of the bed

*****x***********xx*********************xxx******* \$\$\$
\$^^^^
^^
^&**((((
((((+++++++++))) *Knives
fall through tables.* Orana leads Suki and I down a long hallway,
where doors appear on either side, and she points to them.

"Open any door, and walk through." She says, and I open one
and walk through, Suki follows closely behind me.

I woke up today, and I was 70 years Old. Only yesterday I was
toiling over the Superman toy, and who the character belongs to,
and who won the checkers game, and my first french kiss, all of
those broken hearts, and getting my license (which I never got).

When I wake up, I'm lying on a rooftop, frozen to death, but
I'm still breathing, (and my head tells me, in my own words, the
people don't call it breathing anymore these days, and I'm stupid
for not remembering to call it Looping because it's the future,
and I'm just an old junky piece of trash).

Tape loops reeling round and round, the same mantra. This is the way I talk to myself these days, if I don't have a drink.

Remember, while I'm sleeping, viewing the naked body from above, Aceo curled in a ring, and I look down at her, there, for what feels like hours, I'm lying here, staring at walls, really, and watching as mist, and cold mixing heat curls together into fog.

Should I even think to get back up again, the walls will spin 80 degrees, and then the walls will turn in on themselves, fold paper first, down onto the ground, fold to crumpled up paper balls, they will bounce, a blue play ball, (streets have done this same shit before: a spring loads up and tensions tighten, and the heavy weight of the plaster sags to the ground, and breaks them up where the wall has crumpled and the plaster falls off in pieces, hurling flecks, and shattered shapes through the small, black spiral. Spinning white lines collide together into the yogurt of the century, where a hole beyond the floor used to be.

I like to watch the dancing tape player washing over the sea-wall, in the torpedo suction of the heavy black hole, and all of me being sucked

Under the ivy

And into the piano skin

Looping over the hot floor, panting.

The singer within my old tin foil body frays, but still it would like the chance to emerge from the stereo in a Cathode-ray, the speakers wired to the radio, and the static news ... But, I lay out on this fucked, aluminum foil roof, and listen to the rain. Someone nearby plays a reel of slow cough syrup out there ... Slow cough syrup songs remind me of them, Wendy and Hi, and Aceo.

I sense an animal in the thicket, an animal who lived here before. Maybe it's Wendy, but we don't talk anymore. She disappeared a long time ago, in the fluids of my body, inching along the vibrations, the...

Casio keyboard stubble itchy back, before the hand in the mirror, faceless detail,

Shaving my beard, I guess it was,   the   ...

Radio, as it wished, shaving away her memory, well not memory, but ...

 Back in time, when I was young, before I had to eat, sleep, think and breathe soup, I was learning skittle skill, Tao, two of me would switch form, lurk around the stereo shop in the mall, one of me was named Early/the other's name was Wendy Brush.

The two of us were inseparable then, literally. It was the bond which could never be severed, without a kind of sad, and seriously invasive brain surgery.

We would chew bubblegum, and take turns blowing bigger bubbles, until (Wendy's usually) one of the walls of the gum popped. She would point out a cute girl. I'd pop.

Hey, Early!

 My teacher Misses Stroke would pull me around a corner of the mall, and start kissing me with her tongue, open mouthed, and pull me further and further away from Wendy, into a dark corner, until she got me up on a ledge, propped me up, and would somehow (slip me backward into a dream), and let me in, through the back window of her house.

The old wood panelling I remember. A small zenith television would always play color cartoons in black and white. I didn't care what Miss Stroke did to me, or what she thought of me. She would pay me a lot, and I could take Wendy to the arcade.

Wendy would finally find us, she'd peak in, blowing bubbles, and point, giggling at naked Misses Stroke.

Giggling was how we dealt with the smells, Misses Strokes pink nipples sticking out, her funny brown pubic hair curled, and flattened from being in the tight underwear all day, doing lessons.

Wendy and I would run a circle around Miss Stroke. Her head with its feathered, mid nineties afro, spun like the girl from the Exorcist, sometimes Wendy just sat back and watched the cartoons and licked her big, rainbow twisty lollipop from the mall, and I'd drift out, through the stereo waves, through the house, to the kitchen sink, vomit purple candy on the plates, all over the knives, spinning round the ceiling fan, around and around, until Miss Stroke got too damn close to me again, and straddled my 'thing' really tight, moaning, and needing full attention from me, and to me, and then my thoughts were not mine, when she whispered.

"You! Stop!" Looking down at me, reading my facial 'diary,' feeling my whole being inside her, she could maybe see Wendy there too, suck me all the way inside her. Eyes, like serpents slither through me, via my thingy already devoured.

Her victim needed caring for, to watch the prey struggle a little longer, cat eyes glaring over from a black hole the size of the clouds. Wendy watching in the other room a cartoon about a giant dog. I remember the smell in her house as we left. I could smell the cotton candy in the mall, and I'd take the money Miss Stroke had paid to keep me quiet about the ordeal, the daily chore. Then, I'd take Wendy to the video arcade.

This memory turns a nail in the wooden paneling of my heart as I escape through the back window, at an older toil ... The room has been abandoned for many years. The old Zenith is still on the bookshelf above the dresser, and the poster of an old red barn in Connecticut, still tacky glued to the wall.

[Wombats! Run thirty laps!]

Oh, the Wombats, everybody loved the Wombats.

I watched from benches with my sony pocket radio, and Wendy Brush. We'd smoke cigarettes and talk about television shows we liked, watch the cheerleaders do toe touches, and leer at the football players.

I was done with all the sexualized social confines at school. Miss Stroke took care of this urge. Somehow everyone at school ignored or condoned sexualizing children.

I was in the front row of the class every day, tortured by sex, so I spun into two kids, one named Early, and one named Wendy Brush. Yeah, I was a disaster, I know but things couldn't get worse, right?

At lunch me and Wendy ate fries with brain cells, I started getting intimate with this cute raver girl named Aceo, she was cool, she turned Wendy and me on to white blotter Acid, white on white, Looney tunes, and psilocybin mushrooms. Magic, she was.

I'd sit there at lunch eating brain cells, scanning the cafeteria like a spy, an agent of the halls, because it's normal to do this kind of thing, and I'd watch as the school mascot (The giant stuffed wombat) walked in through the gym, the big purple fuzzy slow motion, slicing off kids heads, and stabbing teachers in the necks. This all appeared in my vision slowed down to a reasonable speed so I could witness every detail of the murders in action. The school mascot who kills, what a trip. Then the blotter would take a turn, and I'd see I was just eating corn on the cob, and the Wombat was giving out high fives to all of the teachers, and classmates.

That year I failed all my classes, and had to be held back. it's when Wendy and I met Hi.

"Hi."

"No, my names actor ally Hi."

"Oh, sorry, Wendy, or Early Brush."

"Brushes?"

"Brush."

"People call me Early though, not sure why. Except, well I don't sleep. could. Be it. You want some acid?"

Huh?No! Drugs? Hi looked around. Hi wore a Navy blue jumper with red and white boy tie, her hair flat, jet black, and under short cut bangs, her chocolate eyes constantly scanned the surroundings. A menacing smile crept onto her face.

"What's acid do?"

We blurred out across the halls, weaving through the marching band players, arm in arm, her clutching tight her science and math textbooks, out the gymnasium, pushing past trombone Suzy, Tubba Mike, Adam the snare drummer, and all the cheerleaders, and the rest of 'em. Blurred together kaleidoscopic blue and white of the school colors, out to the cafeteria, where I introduced Aceo, who was sitting eating her lunch alone.

"Hi, this is Aceo, Aceo, Hi."

"Hi." Aceo said, her pink lipstick and silver painted teeth glittering back and forth in Hi's little drooling vision.

"Ac-eo, whoa." Hi was entranced like I still was.

"We're going out to the track, behind the football field, you wanna go?" Aceo said.

"Yeah, I guess." Hi said, clutching her science books tight, in order to block her small chest from my gaze.

[Fast forward, to the party at Maria's]

I got a big bottle of cough syrup before the party so I was fucked up and stumbling around like a real loser should look, with my NyQuil, Robitussin, whatever shit Wendy found at the corner store, clutched tightly in my grip. Wendy had a forty of Steel reserve, and kept handing out sips of it to the jock boys who she, I guess, thought were cute. Little did they know what was in the forty. Shhh! Surprise!

So, I guess from the outside view it looked like Early Wendy brush was double fisting it tonight; a forty oz of steel reserve, dosed with secret sauce, and a bottle a cough syrup. Classy, at the age, I knew I was fucked for life pretty well after the night, would I ever be the same? I had figured out I was dying a year ago, out on a mushroom trip through the dessert in a minivan the summer before, packed wall to wall with hippy freaks.

I just needed a cigarette and the party was complete.

"Hey, turn up the stereo. Oh wait I brought my own! Wendy, crank it to eleven!"

O.   Tell me the length

T. KCAB NRUT < Upside down

Umber car, our umbrella,

Umbrella, that's a cat

Like special, demolition of

The old library-

[Paper power lines out keep take off not sure, hallway still many out]

Sending in thickets Crayola

In an echo chamber — surely wear

shoe no.1 in a landslide, up to your

 old ear in video crayons,

Yelping, melted yellow ceiling

> Yubbah
>
> Scuba
>
> Dubba

When I came to in the parking lot of the 7-11, my body had been soaked in something resembling gas. Or maybe I perspire a lot.

> wall entry way   - The rafters

Are forks [dangle bananas,]

Flames ahdkj   wooden table like train tracks

To the before in a basket,   holding

Flash cards,

That night Wendy and Hi, and Aceo and I start doing meth a local street kid sells to us for three dollars behind the dumpsters at the 7-11.

[Fast forward to graduation]

[Fast forward to college]

[Fast forward to my first job]

[Fast forward to getting fired]

[Fast forward to sleeping outside of the post office.]

[Fast forward to marrying Aceo, and Hi.]

***

Bananas hang melted black over my room, I'm 70 now, lying in a coma on the stereo-plastic rooftop. Hi, Wendy and I got married, now we clutch heroin 'caps' under waterfalls, barely able to light the tin~

Aceo has a show on the radio every friday. We go over there, and through the radio speakers, we can touch everyone around us, and it's how I can be close to them. We sleep in the radio stations green room, and Aceo almost loses her job. Those old times, I toil in, the bells play, ringing in the stereo, the circuits are fingers, and all I can think about is Barley growing slow-mo. I am in my bed in a field of it; in a field next to me in my bed, my bed posts tall as the barley. Bed in the middle of the field, and Aceo and Wendy and Hi and me are all together, snuggled up to each other in our secret field, smoking cigarettes like in school out on the track. A Sheet of snow thrown over a white Sheet, over the grey sheet, over the bones emerging bones, and guitar speaking the body referring to The body_____
_____> Sheets of glass, ice falling over us, in the bed, soaking into us, love those wobbling forks in the bananas, trying to eat, our hands shaking violently, covered now in wateR, the field floods green, we are now underwater. Our bed is covered with snakes, with glowing fish, splashing morning up, as the bed floats up to the surface, and wakeful, our collected belief we breathe, and swallow. The bed floating down along the river, across the ocean, entering Thailand, then China, then India. We smoke slow lungs full of toxic chemicals, kissing, Hi and me. Blurring like school, in this turbulent sea.

"Federico!" Tuned in to slow drift, I see the fox eye ... Purple blurs across my old toil, self esteem and complexion of rose blush on my cheeks, the radio plays as Hi and me kiss and smoke, traveling around in our bed, crossing jungles, splashing off of waterfalls, Wendy steering the bed, here I flee the "storm," Crossing over, I am old now, I toil too much, I am Striped in white gloves Wishy ... Washy ... Wishing ... Balance, the toe twist like headaches: sugar cubicle design.

"Click one!" Wendy shouts, laughing. I wake to her beautiful voice.

" brown ... cancel brown ... candy toothache turns to THC."
Hi says, laughing at me waking up on my white bed.

Counterbalance-equilateral-   mountains-glass-wing-heavy
win/win - I Elbow around the sheets, smile a little smile.

"I see your teeth." Hi says, and kisses me. It is night, my back
to the waterfalls. I must have traded someone something useful
to have my pockets so full.

This is real life now. I keep telling myself . Waves crash over
the bed, warm, while fish twirl around in the waters, they are
like thin floral arrangements, (thin forks twisted) maybe crabs? I
see below the waterfall, under the black murk, a satellite shuttle
under there, deep, and lodged away, hidden. I angle my wrist,
slope fishing a line through the water, hearing whistle and flute
singing on down a long row of waves, the air rising frozen from
the stream like glaciers, a sculpture full of circus clowns, rising
through underwater clouds of rose colored ice water, undulating
to distant paper piers.

Water's like flimsy rouged twilight, distant undulating roses
... Floating out on blackened waters, for the clouds parting with
black forever, dysfunctional just as momentary glimpse, but followed, and watched closely. A sunrise of our blending bodice
interface, substance, with gloomy peach colored dress, spun
into the waves, iron rows of cabinetry, our voices. My body,
sphere, my body, phone number, elbow room, and eating sparks
like food ... [we emerge on our bed into caves, the libraries of
forgotten history]. [Where we leave our separate selves on the
beach there, united, and then untied, wandering lonely among
ruins, our lost library of long water eroding thee old shoppes
step, elevated now, a signal carries us along through the black
cave, lets us down onto some faded steppes, where we find boxes and boxes of recorded tapes and buried books in the ground.]

Banana Camera

This morning at The Breakfast Table, Orana And R(ei)ka and Suki we're discussing the differences between a Polaroid camera©®™ and a banana, when, I came up with the idea we should put the two together so the Polaroid camera©®™ would (instead of Polaroid film©®™) spit out perfectly ripe bananas into the room. But then the exact structure we would have to sort out. If we were able to do this I would start to feel funny, you know, like I was going bananas. We might actually be going crazy I told Orana, and then she said: well, maybe the Polaroid camera©®™ spits out Polaroid photographs of bananas so if I took a picture of you it would just be a banana, and if you took a picture of me it would just be a banana. Thousands of bananas, put together to make one person out of bananas, and I thought well it's a good idea. Maybe we could actually have a banana camera©®™ so I went into the living room and I drew a picture of the camera spitting out a banana. I wrote on the drawing this: we need to invent a banana camera©™. With a little poorly drawn diagram of a polaroid camera spitting out the banana, and next to it I wrote: "Spits out bananas, we've gone completely bananas."

And then at the bottom I wrote: "Write a poem and a story and an essay about the banana camera©™. And so the banana camera is born. I'm also thinking about having a designer build for me a model banana camera©®™, and I would like a licensed engineer to build for me, and me alone, well them too, this surreal device. But, I don't exactly know anybody who does this kind of thing but I d☐o know some graphic designers who may take some interest in the idea simply as an idea for a sticker or a t-shirt or a hat the banana cam TM copyright 1984 Brave New World Scattergories laughter copyright 1985 1986 1987 sorry I have ADD Batman, because I grew up in the 90s and we like to make t-shirts and hats and stickers of banana cameras™ and things of this nature capitalizing off of the idea which is surrealism. The Lobster phone of the Great Da Vinci or whatever his name was, (haha just kidding) I have ADD, what's his name, what's that dude's name? Grumble, grumble, grumpy pants? Grumble, grumble … Salvador Dali! But, I think he made like suits and he did all kinds of things that he probably could capitalize off his own inventions, but, he's still one of my favorites the realest sir realist whatever. I have ADD. Back to the banana camera©®~~™ the banana camera© will fly on wings and spit out photographs of bananas onto the horizon in a western, like a western story … There's going to be Cowboys and Indians fighting in the middle of the desert over Polaroids of bananas that are spitting out of the sky and the Indians are going to kill all the Cowboys in my story and the Indians are going to kill them with bananas they're going to throw bananas at the Cowboys and in my story and Suki's story, and Orana's story, and R(i.e.)ka's story, and my friends story…we're gonna use the banana camera™© so it can be able to walk with legs and eyes and play guitar and knows how to play guitar really well and spits out pictures of bananas on to the crowd when it's on stage and then back to the Western age. Riding a stagecoach, Cuz' stagecoaches are the thing in Westerns ... The banana camera ©®™is going to be amazing it's going to be about Cowboys being murdered with bananas violently murdered with bananas by Native American people in the story. ~~~this story will be told to every High School Junior, first grade history class, instead of this old shit. It will tell the story about the Indians winning the war against the Cowboys by killing them with bananas, and the inventor of the banana camera will be named whatever name I choose and whatever name Orana chooses, but for now I will call them 12 volt Bolt so it's kind of like Batman from outer space with, with the purple hair and green tongue and looks and listens to Kiss the band, and watched the movie spinal tap one time, and volt bolt plays guitar really, really good with banana camera and then they go to the saloon and make sweet, sweet love 2 the women's running the saloon and they all hang out at the saloon together making sweet, sweet love and then people from the tribes come and live with the women in the saloon and they teach them how to make mushroom tea and mushroom tinctures and pot tinctures ...

A poem about the banana camera:

The sky was oh so full of rock and candid light of snapshot Polaroid film drupes and drips and blobs like little liquid linseed oil lacking Loco Lobby Doozy Do and into the air we saw a swallow was it a bird no was it a plane no it was banana camera come to save the day and in the windowsill of loopy long hair locks and orange peels the scattered crane of Windex splashing on the electric outlet for a spritzer to the dorky little man walked along the sidewalk alone thinking in his mind of the banana camera as it flew through the sky with the birds in the birds and the bees

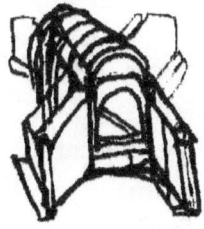

Suki takes me down to the forest where the boys park their ford trucks, and points out the blue ford Billy drives. I shudder, and cringe, pulling myself inward, in fear of Billy.

"He's gone." Suki says, pointing to the rust on the edges of the car. I see vines have been growing through the chassis, and tires from closer inspection are flat, and warped. The front windshield has been shattered long ago, and the seats inside are covered in a thin layer of moss. She points at a hole in the floor, where a small tree is making purchases.

I remember the first time I saw this car as it drove down the ravine. The mud sucking it in, the day I saw it without a driver. Suki wanders up the path, away from the car, and gestures for me to follow her. She smiles.

"I want to show you something."

"Okay? Where?" I ask, quickening my pace. I grasp her thin hand in mine, and we wander along the misty river cut through here, over a log-bridge, to the ancient forest. We wander for some time, floating above the surface of the forest floor, and get to a clearing, where a hollowed out cedar tree hangs broken down, like a crumbled marble statue. She climbs in through a hole in the base, and wanders up, to the first row of branches.

"Come up!" I hear her voice echo. "Come on." I hurry forward, and carefully take through the base, inside of the tree. A set of hand built steps have been built, and I take them up, along the trunk, where Suki is. She is sitting there on the first row, fingering with a rope swing, which connects to a line she tightens, and ties to the cedar.

"Come on." She says, and balances on the rope, tightrope walking across the forest, into a distance away.

"Where are we going?" I shout. I try the rope, and am surprised to feel so light and comfortable, balancing on it.

"This isn't hard." I shout, feeling like a child again.

"Yeah it's easy, come on."

We tightrope walk to a tree, deep in the forest with a house built into it. The roof is slanted to the ground in an a-line, and the walls are rounded, like they are made of clay. The windows are round as well, and I see a light coming from them.

Suki lands down on the porch hanging over the side of the house. Below is a blur of hundreds of feet, before the floor of the woods.

I land down, and we hug.

"I wanted to show you this place." She looks out over the tops of trees, through the mist, at a mountain far down. We stand on the porch for a long time, and she just hugs me, and I feel at peace, finally.

I don't know if I have died here, or if death is even real? I may have always lived in this state between life and death, where there is no beginning or end to my being.

I know , like me, the point of light from where the path unfolds, there are other paths to other places, where I have chosen to walk, instead of this path. Like me, the others (the branches) of my being searches out from this point, making decisions to follow what path they will. Someday, I will meet them, myself, and ask them what their journey was like.

When I try to remember my childhood, the pieces of fragmented color film run in and out of my vision. I see my backyard, the old fence, and a blonde child, behind her is the sun and blue skies. I can feel the warm energy of the sun on my skin. I can smell the grass beneath me. I say nothing, and train my tongue in garbled motions. Is this my memory I see in my vision, it is not familiar to me? It is warm, and I feel good thinking of it. But this has never happened, I'm sure of it. What I am imagining is truly a lie I tell myself. I've lived so many different lives, one me grows old and dies, lying on a bed floating down the river, and, at some point the river leads to the ocean. The other me stands in a forest, next to Suki, my beloved.

"Pull in the rudder, do west!" Aceo shouts to me. I turn and look at her, standing there in a pirates cloths. She looks filthy, in rags, like she has never changed once. The sea laps up around us, rolling huge waves into the bed. Wendy chugs a bottle of red wine, and laughs, imitating Aceo, by pointing her fist in the direction of west with authority.

"Onward! Ho!" I slur out, drunk, twisted, high as a kite in the sky. The edges of the sea fold out forever around us. Wendy hands me a periscope, and I extend it. An island floats in a blurry visual inside the scope.

"There's an Island!" I shout.

"Where!?"

"Up ahead, east to star board, headboard, whatever... West to bedpost!"

"Onward, to the island, there, somewhere, yonder! Over there!!" Wendy drunkenly points in several directions, aimlessly.

"Yes, On ward!" I shout.

"To the Island!" I slurp down the dregs of something awful, maybe wine, maybe liquid morphine, I curl up, recoiling in a horrid fetal position. The ocean slams against the back of the bed, and salty water pulls me out of my coma.

"UGH! What the hell is this?" I hold up a clear, orange bottle of red liquid. A prescription label is printed onto its side. I try to focus my eyes, reading it.

Wendy and Aceo laugh, and spin the bottle of red wine back and forth, until Aceo gets wobbly and falls off of the side of the boat.

She holds the bottle up, out of the sea water, and Wendy grabs her arm, pulling her with me assisting as best I can in my stupor. Aceo, soaked, laughing, climbs back up onto the bed, and shakes off the water, like a dog, soaking us.

"When are we getting to this damn island!" I grumble. Aceo has a strange smirk on her face, and looks at Wendy and then back at me.

She smiles an interesting smile, and then jumps up suddenly, and pushes me into the water, followed closely behind by Wendy, and herself.

"Aif? Do you like it here?" Suki asks. We are curled inside somewhere, it was growing dark, I think we are inside of the treehouse, by the way the windows are shaped.

A soft warm fire burns next to us in a large, handmade clay oven.

"I am Happy with you." I say. Looking around, I start to make out the room more, the hand made table and chairs, the book shelves full of volumes. The small kitchen, and bed, and wooden slat floors, lead up to where I am laying next to Suki, on a soft rug.

"This place is marvelous." I say at last, Suki smiles. I see her eyes are pinched tight, her face holds true happiness in it.

"Isn't it wonderful? This is a gift to you, from Orana and me and R(i.e.)ka."

"You built this?"

"Yes, we all did."

"It started when you left, but it is useless to keep track of when it is, or was, or will be. I wanted to build you a home, where you could come to, if things started to get too confusing, and it will always be here, in whatever time line your body traces out, no matter what world you find yourself lost inside of."

I lay here, soaking in these words of Suki's. Her sentients feels so real, and for a moment I begin to grasp her in my mind, her meaning in my life.

"How will I find it?" I say to Suki.

She points to my chest, and there is a small clasp around my neck, a thin metal pocket watch.

"Here!" She opens the watch, and it spins, slowly, adjusting to a number on its face.

"Look inside yourself, and find who you truly are. The body carries the soul. But the soul is not the body. The spirit wants different things from what our bodies crave."

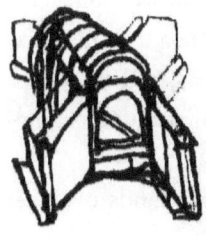

The waves crash over our heads, my drunken high blur of bubbles and water, and hair of Wendy and Aceo create the illusion I am drowning. I can't breathe, I can't breathe! I try to cry out, but the salt water piles into my mouth in a jet stream of chaos. Aceo crashing down, and Wendy floating off into the dark. I struggle up to the surface, pull in a large breath, and scream out.

My toes touch the sand beneath. And I push up, screaming out at Aceo, who is drunkenly stumbling away, toward land. Wendy, Laughing, pulls up the bottle of red wine full of sea water, and sadly pours the liquid out into the ocean.

"Oh, our wine!" Aceo shouts from shore. She is rigging the bed to the sand, tugging on the stand , and falls backward.

"You almost killed me!" I shout, Wendy laughing, pushes me a little, and I swing back, aggressively missing her by a long shot.

"You're fine!" She says, stumbling off toward shore, me following behind her, my head down.

"Assholes…" I grumble, and then laughing.

"You Assholes!" I shout, shaking my fist.

"You guys! Look at this!" Aceo Shouts, pointing into the bamboo trees. Above, in a coconut grove, I see it.

"What is that?" Wendy squints, covering her forehead with her left hand.

"It looks like some kind of house, up in the trees." I shout.

"Someone lives here." Aceo mutters. The waves crash down on the shore, threatening to pull the bed back into the ocean with each of it's tugging currents.

"I never want us to lose each other again." Suki says. She curls up, and lays on top of me, so I can stare straight at her face. Her hair land's down on both of my shoulders, and she wraps herself around me, tightening. I smell the soft scent of chamomile, then cedar.

"Mmm, you smell good." I say, turning my hands over her waist, and settling them there.

"I don't know how to feel," I say, "it's difficult for me to feel good about anything, to let go, and fully enjoy, even this moment."

She sighs, and holds my arms within hers.

"This is because you are used to things going wrong. You are not prepared emotionally, or spiritually for something good to happen, just something terrible." She lays there speaking and I watch her from above her head, her hair black, shifting as she talks.

"I suppose." I say, defeated. She is right.

"Your spirit is strong, Aifrean. You will learn to love again." She adjusts her weight, and lays back on my chest.

"If I love, will I weaken myself to them who try and tear me apart?" I mutter. I adjust my hand around her waist again.

"Thinking of all the worst things, you still have control over The thought, and thought creates the world. It is yours to decide on, whether you allow it to grow, or destroy it from its roots, this is up to you." She says.

"Well, then I will destroy it."

"That is yours, and only yours. We can help you only so much. The world we all create together, crashes into itself in many different ways, you know?" She says.

"I created the town of Billy. A long time ago. It is my world I am responsible for."

I abruptly try to get up, but her weight barely shifts.

We pull the bed by its posts, onto the beach, struggling to get it through the heavy sand, and Wendy grabs the bottle of sailor Jerry's, and cracks it.

"Anyone want a sip?"

"I do." I grumble. Aceo turns and puts her hand out into the air.

"Gimme."

We each take a long pull, and Aceo fingers out a wet cigarette from the bed. The tobacco stains the paper, but she gets it lit somehow. I don't see her use a lighter, and I don't question it either. Just put out my hand like she did and say: Gimme.

Aceo snarls, and hands it over, and I take three puffs and Wendy grabs for it.

"Where'd the pills go?" Aceo says, brushing and fumbling over the sheets of the bed.

"Pills."

Wendy smokes and hands the cigarette over to me.

"I got 'em." She says.

"Why would you let them kill me?"

Suki is quiet for a long time, and then I notice she is crying.

"I wanted to have some control." She whispers finally.

"Control, over what? My life, Suki?" I push her off of me, and grudgingly, stumble to my feet, her hand is thrown up before me, and it's the last thing I see before she evaporates, clean away into the room. The crackling fire pops, and I fall to my knees, confused. My face tightens, and my throat clenches back the urge to sob.

"Suki." I let out. As I say this, I think I hear her, like it's over a telephone, a voice in my ear saying: I can hear you. A whispering, and my hairs on my neck stand up beneath my shirt.

"Who's there?" I whip around, to the book shelves, and scan the volumes quickly, in haste. "Is it you, Suki?" The fire crackles, and pops. My senses are heightened, and I thrash my way through the room, lunging and stopping short, pausing, and listening for the voice.

"The rope there, yeah that one! Pull it!" Aceo shouts, she nudges me to take the long rope hanging next to her head.

"Here, take it." I pull on the rope and Wendy holds me steady on her shoulders,

"You got it, you got it? Dude, your heavy, mother fucker!"

"Almost.. got it." I try through my drunken Codeine blurred vision, to tangle my hand around the bottom of the rope, but it keeps flowing throughout the air away, away.

"God damn it, fucking rope!" I get a purchase on it, and tug as hard I can muster.

"Pull it, hard!"

There on the bookshelf, a volume sticks out a little, one which draws my eye, and I lunge over to it, grabbing it up, in tern the shelf rumbles, and rolls back along a track of some kind, and opens into a chamber inside of the tree where a series of steps spiral around to a dark area below.

"Hello?" I question, shouting into the darkness, my voice stays close to me, insulated in the cedar trunk. I go into the chamber, looking briefly down the steps, and pop my head back into the house, looking around for Suki. The fire goes out a little, and I wander back in, looking over my shoulder at the open room. I stuff a few logs into the fire, and wander back into the chamber, taking the first step down.

"Suki?"

"Are you down here?"

"Suki?"

I hear a banging on the bottom of the steps. And a loud voice, cursing, and then another and another.

"You shit! Hand me the bottle!"

"Hello?" I hear a voice up stairs, on the top floor. It sounds to me like a child's voice.

"Hey, hello, we ah, just arrived from the sea!" Aceo shouts, we are sorry to have bothered… "

"Oh shut up!" Wendy shouts.

"Don't listen to her, she's drunk as a skunk, let me tell you."

I walk down slowly, careful of my step, since the bottom is very dark, and I can barely see down into it, but only hear those strangers voices.

"Um, I don't know who you are, but I'm going to try and come down. I've never been down here before." I utter.

"Never been down here before, isn't this his house?"

Wendy questions, turning up her face like she's got something nasty in her nose.

'This is weird."Aceo Shutters, "It's getting very cold in here."

"I'm drunk,"

"I can't see!" The voices shout. I take a few more steps down, and land on a base floor, and look around in the darkness. But see no one there.

"Hello?" I shout, "Where are you?" I let my eyes adjust for a moment and I still make nothing of the people. I walk around in a circle and the room is empty. A crack of light passes through the cedar, and I wander over to it, and peer through the crack.

The forest canopy can be made out, high up in the tree.

We make our way up to the top of the stairs, and peer into a room, with a fire blazing. There's a white rug, and a bed, and a kitchen, but the child we heard is not there.

"Where'd you go?" I say.

"Hello?" Aceo shouts. Wendy sits down on the bed, chugging the Sailor Jerry's.

"Little bugger split! Wanna sip?" She holds up the bottle, gestures to Aceo, over and over until Aceo shouts.

"What?"

"Ciggy." "Gimme."

"Hello." A voice interrupts from the corner of the room.

A girl in japanese dress stands proper, crossing her arms over her pelvis in a kimono.

"I'm Suki-san." She says.

"Hello, sorry, we thought we heard a child," I say.

"Sorry to intrude, but we just washed up here on this island and…"

"No problem, this house is a safe place for travelers of all kinds."

Suki says.

"Oh, thank god," Wendy lets out, spilling some rum on the sheets of the white bed. Aceo Lights up a cigarette, and Wendy scrambles over to her for it.

"Sorry about my friends, we are kinda intoxicated."

"Fucking Drunk!" Aceo shouts, "Ahoy!"

"Yes, Ahoy." Suki says.

"Suki, I am…" I reach my hand out to shake.

"Aifrean, I know. It's fine, sit. Make yourself at home."

"Oh, thank you. Yes, Nice place, wow! What a beautiful home you've built. Here!"

"Yes, We had help." She says.

"Sit."

I start to feel awkward anyway, standing here, throwing my drunken arms this way and that. And so I sit down on the bed with Wendy. She passes me the bottle of Rum and cigarettes, and I look at her eyes, almost like the first time. Her makeup is rubbed aside, like she has been crying.

"Where's the kid?" Aceo says to Suki.

Suki looks around the room, and holds up her hands.

"What kid?" and then she laughs, "I don't know who you could mean."

"I feel like I've met you before." I spit out, closing over the flame of the cigarette, and allowing my head to flop there, drunken.

She walks over to the book shelf doubled as a door, and closes it, inserting an old volume into a slot that had been lying on the floor.

"People have many faces." She says, finally. "Maybe I look like someone else you know."

"Yes, maybe, sure." I smoke the rest of the cigarette, and stand up, almost fall over, and stumble to the outside, where the trees blur together, and I catch my hand on the railing, throwing up off into the distance, some hundred feet down, the vomit lands in some leaves, and passes through others, hitting the ground floor.

"Fuck!" I hack up the flavor of morphine and red wine, and cigarettes. I lean there for a while, staring off into the blurred together canopy below, swaying, just listening. Feeling my balance drift, and then come back to straight. My body feels ancient, like a crumbling statue, heavy and awkward. I'm starving, I suddenly notice. My stomach after vomiting has been emptied, and I don't remember the last time I ate. I hear the voices of the girls chattering behind me. And the voices slowly dwindle away.

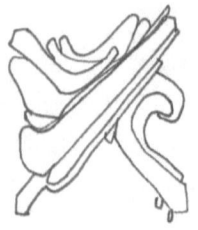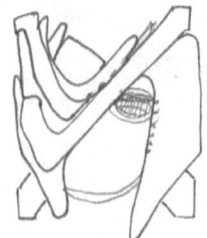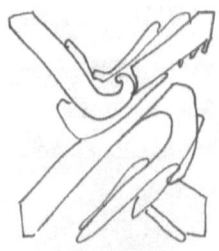

When I get to the top of the stairs, I see the wall of books has been pushed back closed, and I pound on it as hard as I can.

"Hey you fuckers! Hey, let me back in!" I start shouting. I can hear the loud drunken slamming voices, and then they pause.

"Hey! Let me back in!" I hear the footsteps of someone stumbling over.

"Hey! I hear a voice in there. The kid."

"What kid?" I hear Suki's voice. A shuffling of shoes toward me.

"Hey! Suki! Let me back in!" After a long silence, I hear the adjustments, the rumbling of the door mechanisms. A sliver of light carves a dull line into the darkness, and I blur my eyes, squinting. I try to adjust my eyes to the light, and cannot, standing here in the doorway. I strain my eyes, focusing, nothing but some white abyss. I step into the warm water, hear the waves far off as they roll slowly in. I walk out to the edge of the reef, and check for creatures beneath, shivering.

"You guys?!!" No answer.

"Hello?" I hear the waves only, they are crashing in the distance, a mile or so away.

"Ahoy!" I hear someone shouting.

"Ahoy matey!" A hundred feet away, I see a bed floating along,

104

over the reef twenty yards. Four people aboard pass a bottle of wine. Suki's there, I search the water again, shivering, and shout back, wave my arms and form a swan, diving in.

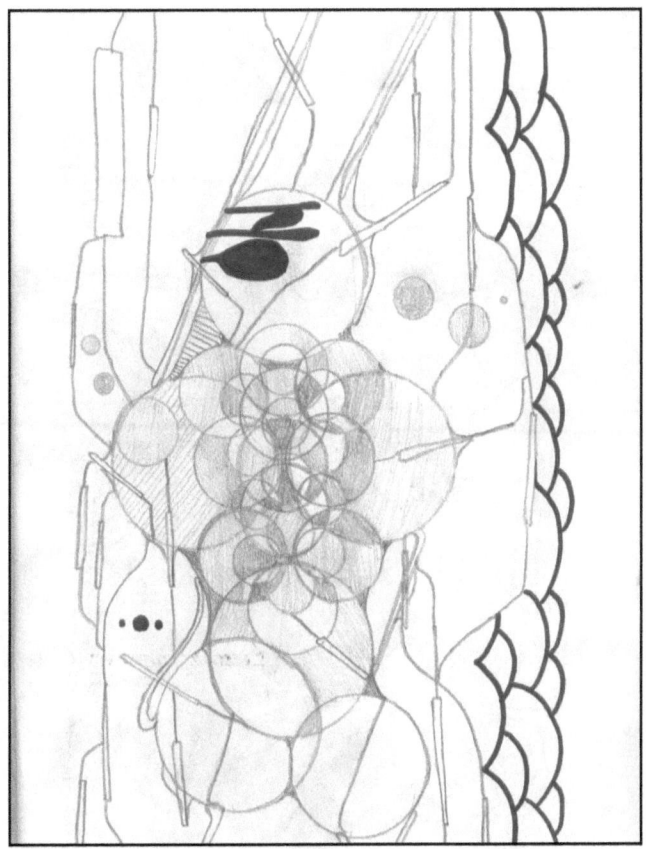

We put on scuba diving gear, and lay out the underwater blanket for our collective picnic. One of you in the audience shouts nonsense, blows bubbles, lucky for the rest of us here who like to enjoy our lunch in peace we don't have to hear you. The ocean is a vast place, a world within a world. The sea operates with its own laws, like pirates do. Big Fish eats little fish. When the blanket folds out I can feel the dopamine pouring plunge, like wine and grass, giddy, I can set the utensils nice, firm but sweet, it's when I'm able to open up enough, and it's when I find the others floating in a bed. It's early yet. It's nice to float around, a little water fountain with angels.

The water is my life.

END NOTES:

(1) Voodoo queen.

Spiritual information blog What are Chicken Feet and Alligator Teeth and Paws used for???~~~~

Published October 3, 2016, Found November 25th, 2018 http://spiritinfo.blogspot.com/2016/10/what-are-chicken-feet-and-alligator.html

(2)Puzuzu

Puzuzu.com

Found November 27, 2018

http://www.puzuzu.com/

(3,4) http://www.puzuzu.com/water.html

Book Two: Transversal

trans∑ver∑sal
(**trans'vərsəl,tranz'vərsəl/**/): Intersecting a system of lines.

Crash

Grizzly makes coffee in the passenger seat, and I'm driving. The bartender gave us a whole big box of rum and whiskey, so we're set for a while.

After the desert disappears, a forest road folds down around us, and the Deville peels through the earth, licking up flames from the soft moss of the street.

Trees pass, blurring, 'til we get closer to California.

'I'm not stopping.' I think.

Grizzly laughs and smokes a cigarette, and we sip Irish coffee.

"A brand new kind of felt has been invented today." The radio blows out like a horn.

"It's uncoiled, and formula."

[Gibberish.] Grizzly flips the channel.

There, at the driveway, a butterfly nozzle collides with the part which

sits nowhere, and Grizzly uses

 Jagged

Winter.

[Am I alive?] The car flips and stays still in mid air.

The Cadillac Deville has us crushed beneath it.

 Grizzly tries rope for our afternoon with Chandelier hands.

All I can think about is all this destroyed free booze, and it is probably what death is, the complete loss. I'm starting to under-stand death more, I guess.

But I feel safe here, we trail down window frames, Grizzly moans low, she is dying probably now. I miss her already.

 The traffic

 transistor, whispering.

Our arms inside of these

  apple trees along with a hidden

orchard.

A sense there, of

 mid future,

draining wind into each other. Grizzly floats up out of the car
first, before I do.

The   Feeling is soft and forgiving, I feel at rest.   The
Deville

   is scattered all over the highway, and cars are crashing in slow
motion into it.

Her and I   found the electric download

         inside of the transmission.

We stagger   over,

picking up in the headphones, back in the desert

   a new satellite.

A soviet segment of the

News.

 Pitched,

broad-cast

         thin lines

and the river.

"This is channel One fifty-one"

"Earlier today Red balloons were found inside of 98-year-old Grizzly Smith Reda. At four-thirty a.m. on the old, dusty highway 85 ninety. The helium of a still inflated balloon was rescued from the smashed ruins of a 59 Cadillac Deville." The news broadcaster mutters.

Lying in front of a radio, crawling insistent into the sunset. 'Her body was a tattered animal, the PICTURE shows this: unicorn, pulled open, and stapled shut. The purple glow of aluminum spatters on the highway. A Cadillac Deville, in pieces next to the body, blackened, ablaze. The wheels spin, radio tweaked, horn blaring.

The victims of the crash floating in mid-air … Spun.

I know I can see past the flipped car, us in the badlands in Nevada …For now, I see just happiness, knowing it, feeling it, knowing we would form some kind of relationship outta string nets, and wire phlegms, and smashed tissue, through all this bullshit, now the helium isn't the main information, like military, a force of etching, the sense of demolition … They would never catch on to the way way way these massive shapes 'orange' and 'fold,' and 'poison' everything. These evil sons bitches never seen a box of jewelry eat your life away! They Coked up, and feeling like anybody else be feeling: the Welsh, German, Irish, Chinese, Portuguese, Spanish, French, African, English … It's hard to describe this feeling, but it's all been done before, Nazi's probably done worse, I despise being here in this feeling with her dead body over there.

Just say 14 karat Gold beneath her (…) you wouldn't know much about this, would you, this kind of image? Those men, they want gold, and they digging inside her, looking for it. What does this say to you?

This question goes out to all those nail gun-slinging amateurs who claim they know my kind. I will rip you open, and solder your wounds closed, look into the crystal ball and see your future. I lit those mother fuckers on fire in a hotel room for raping Grizzly and I. You won't see them anymore, unless you watch the news, the man running out of the inferno, desperately trying to rip off his clothes as his skin folds away in sheets... He lands bouncy on the sidewalk where it lays him to waste. Tell you what I have done, but I will show you my hands. Look at my hands! Do you see anything?

Didn't think so. You just see your own hands. I wonder who you are?

All I see is her hands, she slides her skinny fists through the old skin of the uni derma horse, a purple light pours through the sky being old as it is, the red turns and white curls uniform in slight drifts.

"Do taxidermy on your own skin, and feel a blurry red trike, motherfucker!" We flipped into the middle of the road, run our old Cadillac Deville off the turnpike, and I think Grizzly and I might have kicked the bucket on accident. I could be wrong, but... I'm turning blue in the windshield, she's bleeding bad, her heads smashed; all this over a systematic week and a half. I hear the horn stuck on, I hear her shaking, twitching, she's dying. What would she need to teach me by doing this? Dying, she's twitching. I'm blue, I'm ruined. I try to lift my hand to my head. The horn is frozen solid.

"Brrrrrrr!!!!" The trees are on the ceiling, pouring down into the room. "BRRRRRmp!!!" The glass is broken. I feel the angel's fucking me, they like us broken like this, in pain like toys, they fuck us hard.

I think it has to do with our ritual; the sacred surgeon imparts physical disaster to her body to check six color challenges, are you able to replace your six arms with six colors?

It's a good question, I think. Even if the other body belongs to the teacher, we still got Blade, and Rush, and Grizzly. We still are healing, and we don't need any talk right now.

[Grizzly? Why...must we ...be... platinum...in the glass

cliff?] I ask.

[You do know we 'here of the sidewalk, part of the road, make up of the cement?]

[Here of the sidewalk, boy toy? Here of the sidewalk, what kind of polyurethane you snorting?...] She's feeling nasty today. I like it. The computer valves pass over our heads, in a spacecraft or a 'cloud.' I knew we'd get out of this somehow. The machinery of the universal eye picks up the old Cadillac, and spins us, vomiting out the side windows, and throws us into the ghetto ass tow yard, where they can scrap all of the metal off of the car, including the platinum.

Digital fingers touch a load of whales on the ceiling of space behind me. The whales are pissed as I feel, and roar loudly, smacking their flippers against the machine arms which lift us up.

Grizzly passes breath through her lungs in a long continuum of cotton clouds, duckling feathers, and finally pear seeds, landing all around the forest. We both fall into the mattress of the car parts and the junkyard, and Grizzly fluctuates between white clocks she finds lying around to hands, and things which look similar. We roaming through a valley of red gloves, it's nice, we both come to... Searching old dwellings, and hatchback cars, and Chevrolets for what Grizzly keeps muttering:

"Unicorn skin..."

I am up for any sign, really. As long as it's... you know... saying what might have just happened, at least an explanation, and unicorn skin seems to be very reasonable for whatever reason. But, the thought seems to erase from the mind, as her face changes into a smile, then flattening the skin with her finger tip, she ignores me and instead sits down in a mud puddle where a fallen tire lies. The window of an old Mercedes is my leaning post, and I reach my hand in and pop the door, sit in the passenger seat, and slam it closed.

She can watch as I sing, and play the radio on the old broken cassette player now. She points at the sky though and shows me guitars flying into our caravan from the distant towns below, and we pass on a conveyor belt. [Slimy right!]

[These things are heavy!] I shout. But she ignores me, and pulls a lute down and plays a few strings with her red gloves, getting blood on the lute.

[You're getting it dirty! You're getting your blood all over it!] I can't stand when things get dirty, blended things, clutter, junk. I hate the clutter of our two lives. When we come together into one, it's a fish fry. It's all dirty now, with our fluids, our noses touching, snot pours from one nostril.

"GET OFF OF ME!" I Shout

"I CANT SILLY! I'm YOU!" She says. I hate when they say that. I need answers. Maybe this means hate is us, our relationship is hate. I don't die for real anyway, I don't believe in death or hate. I think I just like things hate, plus, I hear hate is strong, and dislike is more like it. So flow like a nose, dislike what you like but this is all we got, so the conveyor belt it is...

The sky is canceled out with trombones, tambourines, and cello sonatas.

Grizzly enters the back of our caravan, through a tomb of books, softly caresses the tips of her fingers across the pages and enters her hands deep into a salad in our small kitchenette. I watch her and follow the path of blood.

"You know the dress is getting really long on you, you might want to cut it," I say. Along comes, a Panda bear, the border collie dog, looks like snoopy, who puts his paws deep into the salad. "Wow, I want to put my hands in some salad now that you did," I say, and get on all fours, put my hands in the salad, and sooth my fingers burnt, blistered,broken, and bruised spots.

"Damn, it's a compound fracture, if I've ever seen one." I lift up my shattered wrist, with its twenty-four slight bone fragments sharply shredded through my skin, and cringe a little as the salad leaf and broccoli scrape a nerve.

"I ain't dead yet mother fucker!" Grizzly shouts. "Come on, Panda bear," she says. "Let's go eat some french fries!" She and the dog leave the junkyard.

The sky rides in on a tricycle at first, pulled by a little white baby in diapers who smiles the biggest, proudest smile. He is pulling a little red radio flyer with him too, getting swallowed into the ether; a little shallow glass pool I use, to look through for viewing…for the alligators, and swans, and the graceful large birds, the pink flamingos, the pandas, ostriches, for the tiny fishes, the green frogs, the snapping turtles, spiders, roosters, dogs, cats, goldfish, rats, snakes, and lamas…

"Those who swim, please swim!" Grizzly shouts, holding up her arms at one end of the looking pool. Through tie-dyed parking garages, and tie-dyed shoes, and socks, and treehouses, and old cars parked in the junkyard with exploded hoods, and cafe's, our old hooptie Cadillac goes spelunk.

I watch, smoking a cigarette, down at old towns below as our caravan passes, stork-ostrich, lion-giraffe, and rat-zebra sticking out their heads behind us in the clouds.

Grizzly pops out of the other side, into a black and white spiral, and smells like patchouli as she rises from the water of the canvas of the sky. She shows off her telephone-flamingoes, and her calm cranes of vinegar, drizzling downward onto the clouds.

Sweet white whispers in the woods pearl about, the spinning yonder wheels of the Cadillac, green of healing voice takes it back on, and wanders off, like a scared momma deer, and we follow.

This is where I jump down, and swim toward them ~ through the blue sky, into the white clouds.

The Russian satellite comes in across

                the new planet, Group 12 discovered and sent

news of, after

exploring   time envelopes, within the

Morva galaxy.

Gallons

of

enamel found

dormant

in rocks,

paper spiders we watch for the first time, com-

ing to life on

an old

Vegetable, we used to call

the   Earth –

I. SEW THE THREADS THROUGH THE SOAP
NEW YORK CITY   2014

Her and I thread it, sew with hands, her tangled, even in electric, neon soap.

At our lab, in the lake beneath the dithering ape hangers all the
way crystal, Grizzly and I make our way to a tugboat thin, blue
christ ~ outside of the arms of a machine reach - once at the
calibration mode, we rest at dawn, the thighs, a propped Usnea.
Our bed makes patient gestures toward one another, even and
soft. Shale, she has found in my pelvis, or glow in the dark pad-
ding under my thigh segments.

I speak briefly of our beautiful-mutation- symphony we are
working on to keep away Vampirism, and she nods, uninter-
ested, but sweet. I miss her, Grizzly.

She holds up a pair of trimming shears to party with, the same
toys

as radios and paintings, we get into, after wet and entangled ~

straightened out of my orange shoulders, she uses a neon inspection device to twist up my brain cells into a baseball field

look on my face~

Darkness follows, and then STATUES.

We ride our white outing boat through the lake, toward our quail statues, quail marble, rains, and memes, honking a floatation situation. I'm turning southern drawl of bicycles, a spinning hand to reach the mathematics, (if there are any under the lake) with the string: white aluminum, wood, American flag, neon pink, and native string, I turn the boat and we are ashore, walking four a.m. The quail are nesting, the whole town of statues forms in one big nest.

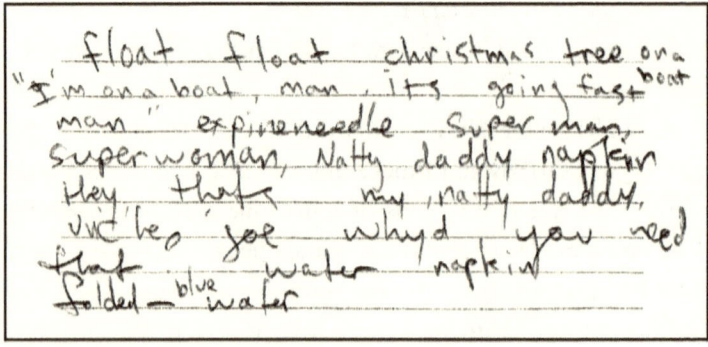

The Difference

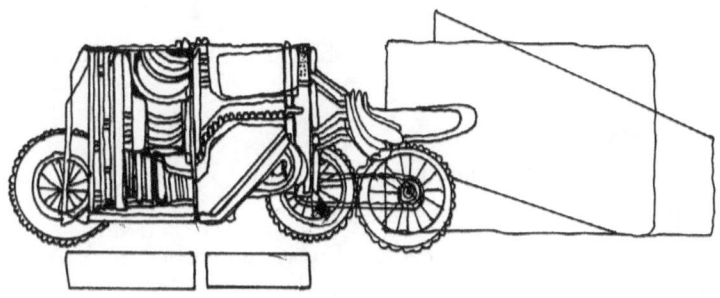

When I photograph Dust, Grizzly writes calculations on a sheet of paper and I tack it up next to a spot on a map.

There is a harsh yellow light which spasms out into section across our station, and we both have to adjust for new-difference-equipment. This is a new thing.

We move our equipment down to the place on the map in a separate boat near the lake.

I should yell something, but I know Grizzly is tired, and we just got her balloons removed so she is a bit sore.

[Pour finish to the table, would you?] She shouts, and so I do, but It's spinning, the liquid finish splashing around in the station. She laughs it off, and I clean it, watching the laquear drip through the floor, under us. The lake is peaceful and it's a nice day to be at the equipment station. Down, into a theater seat, the two of us sit, enjoying a cigarette each.

[You know, this place puts me in a peaceful mood.] She says, sucking on the smoke, and then blowing it out smooth.

A witness watches a clothesline turn in circles. We laugh, and she thinks he's got Aspergers or autism in some form. As the ship drifts down, the white boy in a white sheet swims under the ship, his shoes falling into the current. His 'oranges' float away and he reaches out to get them.

I watch through Grizzly's flame-red marker, she brandishes over, case in hand.

The pterodactyl devours the white skin of the boy, and we laugh a little.

[Poor guy, huh?]

[Yeah, serves 'em right.] I say, shrugging.

[I hate humans, they're a disease.]

[Yeah, but she never gets full, I worry about her. She's like a bottomless pit.]

The torn body below is being thrown into the air like the pterodactyl is playing with a toy.

She starts to mutter to herself, unaware ~

[I saw rolled-up rugs in the garbage. It's freezing, snowing.] I'm pondering this to myself, in my mind. I watch the version of myself lying in a pile of naked girls, we're all making snow angels. [This's better.]

I see a badge covered in blood hit the window of the ship. Another cop is eaten in half and another.

[They musta called for backup.] I say taking a soft puff from my cigarette and then exhale it softly.

[Well, more for her. I guess.] Grizzly smiles.

After we get our daily work finished up, Grizzly takes me to a show at a plush, red theater. We sit down in our seats and relax.

It smells like popcorn. On stage, they have built these giant paper houses. The walls flow, with a fan, or seemingly by our Galaxy fan. A painted backdrop made from the garbage rolls around on skates and the theme music blasts like a circus side-show.

Some stagehand in the back releases a squawking group of flamingos into the audience void. Other characters at random appear above, floating charted waters, displayed, there, I focus maps on a video projector ~ rolling from my seat the footage of turtles.

White telephones are being lowered to our seats from above, in the rafters, where I see men rapidly untangling the chords before the whole room goes black.

[BEEP BEEP BEEP BEEP.]Echoes through the room

"Sisters Forest" is carved into a lit sign above the audience.

[I could lounge around in the corner with gold hand links, connect all of these branches to chandeliers,] A voice mutters, the speaker blasts the sound into the crowd, and everyone begins to cheer for some odd reason.

[So many times a day I want to take down, from the top shelf, a box full of masks in fallen branches, and teach a small group of children before they lose their minds, I would teach them how to fly~] The voice mutters. I can hear the sound of his cigarette he puffs between a vowel.

I roll up the rear window, and we putter off, over the lake, back to the base.

[I liked the telephone thing they did.] Grizzly says.

[Yeah, Me too, it was cool.]

123

Ashley comes back to the station from wherever she has been, she rides in on her crystal substrate, a formed shard of quartz crystal with seat and hovering capabilities. Hunched back on the door jamb of straw, in her shitkickers, she fills up buckets of the lake on her way up to us.

Grizzly is chewing a long length of the straw, she points in the direction, where

big wooden boats - made of crushed chairs - dock in the harbor.

[You see those broken chairs down there, docking?] Her remarks to Ashley are like loops, or frogs, jumping from the shore to lily pads. Stuffed from the pizza we ate, she sits; proper in a lime green chair, Grizzly does.

[They are the guests, everyone please be friendly.]

A herd of small, white cows tramples through the shallow water onshore, they hang their heads to drink.

Grizzly hands me a lantern in our cotton hammock.

Later, Ashley is filling the room with chairs. I nudge Grizzly and yawning, ask what she's doing, with my eyebrows.

[Ashley, break out the loom.] Grizzly says.

[Let's make sure our guests are comfortable.]

The girls do twelve loops, Grizzly wanders ropes with Ashley, jammed up with half-broken chairs. I fall asleep in the hammock. In my dream I see a connective tissue, all black thread turning in my eyes, coming together in a knot. Lurking in the black room, made of threads and knots, invisible typing is noticeable in my mouth. I taste stripes of thin liquid, peels of grapefruits over my tongue, drip Football games onto a television set, flickered off in the lake distance.

Grizzly installs her beautiful telephone cables around my head.

I leaf through old papers in the attic. The times, Anemic, phone busters, word maps, I chew a stick. Secretly, I am calm, but it looks like I'm angry, on my knees in the dust meditating.

3

The mixture of powdered algae, from a basket, lowers to my theater seat.

The whole theater goes flooding down beneath the lakeside.

We lay our separate bodies across the Flatrock, a red theater of flies comes into view here, above me. Pills dip from the sky to our relaxed lips, a thumb and a string elaborate, we take a break, stop, feel a moment of elegance. We both share well, this dream.

4

When entering unheard voice, the signature of a shallow light is involved.

She sneaks into my lodgings and crawls up to the hammock I'm now in, sleeping ~for a pinprick of soil, I trade her one parcel for a gateway, and taming electricity, now floating alone with dolphins, in an ocean we bore

simple blue breath into the sand, the one eating the sky, we drift together.

5

Under a passage of chests, we glide, dangling vinery sifts along with the algae when our little freckled friend appears, un-announced.

Alloy sags in the archway to the tunnel. Burs cling to the socks and leggings, a rather well-placed focus of sunlight eats away at the clouds ~ an undulating mass shines candle wax at thin storms ~

6

Grizzly and I hold hands on the shore of the lake and watch as a hundred cellophane three-piece suits hang at the beach, sifted of gold in the water. With information, carving out, we see lists coming from in the pockets.

According to these lists, food is to be purchased.

TV jargon starts up over the noise of voices, our tongues start flapping, the lake is bubbling up books and pianos begin to surface.

7

I sleep in an outfit Grizzly had sewn together out of white leather on her Bell & Howell sewing machine. Songs play for me, my breakfast.

Wires carve mechanically through the far wall next to the picture frames, into the refrigerator, until it hollows out one side of the wall. Samples of hair fall out from the hole in the wall and onto the floor.

A quick freeze swoops through the room, beneath, I smell a faint

Perfume. Grizzly opens her mouth and leans back in her chair, indulges in a shadow, as I inspect specimens from beneath microscope. Very small hearts appear under the lens, across the edges of the sample: Little hearts. Later, I sing to the birds by the river, and walk a mutated experiment (an experimental, drugged body I have made from scraps) on down through the ferns, by the lake. We take the body through a garden bed of sound waves, the three of us clutter up at the tree line for an hour, to make repairs on this new experiment. Grizzly's breath shows in this cold - A fresh snowfall makes the temperature drop. I work on the experimental body in the snow, pulling out gears, and cleaning them, and then replacing them under lantern light. Soft flakes land on my shoulder as I do this.

A pencil costume dives into the water next to us, this guy's been wearing his costume everywhere. I can't go anywhere without bumping into him, but no one else seems to mind or notice him.

Grizzly makes paper snowflakes, coughing night into a small Sake Cup.

Her and I watch the lake, turning into a seven in the snow with ice.

After an hour, she and I are snowed in with the drugged body, and the pencil swims in circles shivering, around and around the lake.

Vague, paper birds are witnessed, as we lay down to make love in the ferns. She arches her back, and relaxes her shoulders on the ground, while I kiss on her vagina. The ash falls over the cliffs of the lake, night falls - Grizzly folds her knees over my shoulder in orgasm. My shadow falls to my side, I see an ashtray beneath her thigh full of cigarettes, covered in blood.

8

Grizzly and I both cum, and smoke bloody cigarettes and then drive through the lake in our Cadillac Deville. We pass a liter of Clan Mccuran Scottish whiskey back and forth and crank The Pogues.

9

I am starting to doubt if I'm even alive at this juncture. When she turns the car and we watch big, heaping piles of garbage flying into the clouds from under the water laboratory, I just drink.

10

My mind is twisted into knots in a roller coaster, and Grizzly is the only passenger aboard, riding the roller coaster over and over. The operator lets her on and pulls the lever. Some child boards the ride, her hair disheveled. The child has just awoken, and folds up crumpled pieces of paper and throws the papers into the air, as they curl along the tracks, going upside down.

[I really shouldn't be drinking.] I mutter.

Ceremony

I cry bottles of pinot noir from above the town, glass beads rain down into toy radios at the harbor, beneath me. Adrift with ghosts, Grizzly looks up as I walk through old rooms, wearing white rubber. I cannot find a start to anything which feels like a maze, like here.

I'm intent on stopping a hunter, who has been killing animals at dark roads all last week, leaving their bodies ripped open, and only apparently taking the hearts.

[If you exist, you exist, with feeling, nervously.] Grizzly mutters, pulling out a heat seeker, and bow and arrow.

We fold into one body, curling into a spinning tornado of skin and hair and bone, crashing through town, ripping up houses, and cars.

We fold together as one, landing near a castle on the horizon. A humpback whale crosses through its front walls and into the clouds.

The castle rolls up in the sea. I listen to the groans echoing through the ocean. The sky is full of lymph nodes and the cherry trees we had planted. Our planet is a strange ghoul and cistern. Oblivion, sweating down a mirror. We are careful, looking for the hunter.

Golden stones merge to gather us together, under Angel's Galion, a withered white lace, and dark wool. Grizzly and I uncoil our arms from each other, unlocking our legs, we spin a web of our bodies through the trees.

Radio waves dangle hats over the Cadillac Deville, after image: the scarlet fur coat like timepiece importance, Arnica for the spine, The air is parsnip, echoing elegance, the forlorn come pleased foam gargantuan.

My hair tries running for the wolves, to back them up from the hunter's bullets. We can only escape by making a path through a window, and the hunter is spotted beneath a pile of clothes, near the outhouse. Her arrow spins through the air in a cutting spark, and the hunter becomes a family of leaves.

Maps are being built in the latex room, by humping nurses. We take our boats into the paper lake, behind the factory, covered from head to toe in sterile bags. The body of the hunter at our feet in the boat is covered in thick blood. Her mouth gaping open.

The rain is unrelenting, it is like the tears of God. We drink whiskey in the back of a brain maze. We're using the hunter's body as a habitat, as it dries above the flames of the fire.

[Love you, need sleep] I say to Grizzly.

[Is it okay, I try to sleep, I love you and I want to talk tomorrow.] She says, drifting off in the human's ripe smell.

I look through the hunter's nostril.

"These people think in a string." I think before drifting back to sleep. What a train wreck, the human head reflects glass Librium houses inside.

In the substation, woven quilts are being washed and hung up to dry.

The British are pulling out their two-way radios and snapping decayed pictures, waiting for the train wreck in the human head to enter the tubes of salty rush, this is code Ashley needs a new skin. Just kidding Ashley. Salamanders crawl along the tile walls/ Part Zero. These humans sickness comes from rage, smells like the floor and marbles into nauseous vomiting.

With hair rising in the stomach to the throat, passengers wait for the glass train to enter the tube.

After ten hours, we wake and drag the hunters dried skin through the forest, weaving pathways through the backyard of our house. Motors are turned on, we plug in the diagram machine, and plug in an apparatus which further heats the skin.

"Their minds are full of roads and houses," I mutter as Grizzly stretches the fresh skin over the pulleys of the apparatus.

This is supposed to be just random, but I cry cherries and diamonds, and I watch the skin dry out. Grizzly collects the tears, and handles them like diamonds, and presses them into a ball jar.

[These tears will be good next winter.] She smiles.

PART ZERO

I go back to bed, I'm planning to float around in my bed in the clouds. Grizzly jumps around in the leaf piles outside. She stands and stares at the sky. I'm going to lay here and wait for some orange juice. Safety comes out from the soil, as she stomps around. In the computer, inside the house plants, comes a nice warm bathtub I dip in and soak through. I hear voices spoken from within the cables of the water. My body loses filth, Grizzly looks through the stars I'm riding through in this bathtub, watches the hunter's blood come away, unstuck from my skin.

The jars of plants are rotating and spilling jars of baby coy fish into the tub, like notes of songs, the music brings a light classical pattern.

Grizzly lights candles when she gets back. Birds carry the candles up to the ledge, and I watch them place down the calm flames onto the edges of the tub.

I see an orphanage in a clearing, and the children carry a coffin, with the soul of the hunter inside. Big bottles of black cherries, the circle with numbers around the coffin, as an offering. Big bottles of black paint are poured over the soul. Some watery chairs are lifted from the lake: name tags, note tags, and price tags snowflake out of the clouds, and the soul changes into seven red balloons, floating up from the coffin.

I set a time bomb on the edge of the hunter's coffin and watch as the coffin is placed in an animal testing lab, where fur collectors gather around to mourn their loss. All of the animals being tested on have escaped from the lab, and are scattered to the woods at the edge of the lake. The lab techs are sobbing for the loss of their hunter. The time bomb explodes. Arms and legs and brains mix into flames. Grizzly must have been busy last night, while I slept.

A half-broken figure is discovered in a box beneath a line of oak trees.

[I want to talk about the chandelier.] I say to Grizzly.

[I'd say bring your bag full of spoons, the one with black cross-stitch, and white leather round the bottom. I'd say a lot of things these days ~]

[Forget the way my voice unfolds, because unfolding things are of a house or a genius. So forget the nonsense.] She says, hunched over the new skin, oiling it.

I am drawing a drunken scribble on white paper with a black sharpie.

[I love you, Grizzly.] I say.

44.7 DNA Radio

Static plays on the radio and I dig out cigarette butts from an ashtray. I hold forks everywhere I go now. Sometimes I put socks on my hands, and hang in the rafters of the cabin, playing hand puppets. The children who watch Izabelle (the pterodactyl) play dice on the beach. I paint my hands and feet all red. I have a face mask I wear as I dig through the trash the hunter had left behind. Everything I dive out I push around in a shopping cart on the ship, and drink beer, smoking cigarettes with my fork hands dialing the tuning knob of the radio.

106.5 Sweet Oldies

I watch bicycles on the side of the mountain, passing with their bird feathers dropping from above. On the ceiling, chicken scratch is scribbled above the tub, all over the ceiling. Grizzly and I are looking on these folks, riding toilets across the mountains, turtles give each other hugs, eyes in their pockets. An elevator is going up and down, up and down. Inside the elevator,

Turkeys eat and climb into the attic. An arm finds a clock in the attic by the Christmas stuff.

[Let's do Christmas in the attic this year!] I shout.

[Okay, whatever.] She says.

107.3 The edge!

I am seeing apparitions of fish across the sky as I walk the streets drifting apart like two sheets of ice back to the base.

Grizzly and I meet at the base, and drive through the lake in the Cadillac Deville, passing a bottle of wine back and forth.

104.2 s m o o t h   j a z z

We follow a waterfall with our clown car and cruise along with an ostrich in the back seat. Flowing over the edge with it, we hold up our hands above our heads and scream with joy. Grizzly is dressed in a skeleton costume, and I'm shivering in a tablecloth. It's Halloween.

Our junk boat is full of turnips and folded clothes, exploding in the water on impact.

[Let's do it again!]

[Yeah!] We fly off of the waterfall again.

The lake emits long, dangling hats, the fishermen of Scarlet harbor hook up from below fish like fur coat fish and timepiece fish. This is an important fact around these parts, see. I'm speaking from my wheelchair on the shore because implanted in replacement, I have an Arnica Spine, see.

I'm watching birds across-shore eating cars, mostly. The boys wave their sloshing beer cans, I don't move, just nod.

They fly their sign in my direction:

NEED BEER. I chuckle and flip them off.

[Asshole hicks.]

The air is echoing elegance~ The waters, flavored bruise-blue~ Tight in my thin tablecloth, careful, watching all-black forms of my peripheral.

On my radio, I listen to Spanish guitar music, and drift off in sleep, sneaking a hat over my eyes.

[Real Mammalia, me.] In my eyes, the lake eats a warehouse, engulfs it in its waters.

Six weeks ago

Grizzly and I wake up under a Cur.tain. We've been watching armchairs yarned in factories all night, as they take away our great grandmother from our room into a ward. They say she be alright, they are going to help her. And then they say she has cancer of the lungs, and is going to die. I imagine a string of long fluid woven into her assembly.

Grizzly tears up, and wraps her arms over my shoulders.

Apt for a tapestry, a long room is woven of her memorized thread of choice, comes into view around the two of us in bed.

[I love you.] She whispers, her tears falling to grandma's sleepy head. A Volta television swamp floats up at each of our merging breaths, gentleman like. I walk her down to the swamp so she can cry. Heated from lengths of rope nerve, her body shivers beneath my hands as six looping pythons swim across the water, curling through the T.V.'s.

I pull out my time keeper and inspect it [4:44] a tilted mirror and a bookshelf float passed, and I snap it shut. ♥:♥♥

"Theatrics doubled (/when spoken to/) fourteen mirrors" The radio blathers.

The radio has gotten into following people through my secrets - I have seen the evidence of other shadows doubled with the voices on the radio, a four head of micron calibrates like a mutated machine hybrid, and splices together with the cells of an armadillo, or a cheetah, the gulping sound of the chain drive dislodges a small door, and I watch Grizzly kaleidoscopic candy from the drop catch.

[Want one?] She offers. I extend my outer arm, and plant my fingers beneath the springs.

Our life grows together in braided hair, challenges, her and I and the Marquis, an albatross found in our new candy equilibrium. Harsh bone sculpted framework moves along the desert floor behind us, puzzle hands fumbling, twinkle down, to plant a Hammond organ. These hammonds begin growing from the dry soil. (hours) of plastic touching together fills the desert, our childhood is filled with lapping Salmon, and the spherical Aquarium there in, like a blooming flower, rises, spinning before us. The fingers of the mechanism play very well the hammond, to spin each half rotation of the sphere open, full of Salmon. The fingers grow ripe, the machine's hands produce potatoes.

A swarm of bees enter a tower, giving birth to crystalline honeycomb.

Grizzly and I walk along the pathway, up to the tower. She mentions at some point the year should be reconsidered, or accounted for by the local accountant.

We perch from a birds nest in the top of the palace in giant rosemary.

Our mice neighbors twinkle in, through our fingers, up along the tree, proposed leaves before them. Long shapes in our hand-assembly connect a three dimensional skyscraper in the tree.

We're shouting, undressing in the projection over the trees, old pin point swing sets sing below the porch,   the   shallow end of the swamp

can be seen from here. Our pearl necklace – connection starting up at our fingers, drips down. Ink warped leaf fabric onto the swamp waters - starting to climb. Somehow, the ink fabric makes its way along the oka trees, beneath, and unfolds, spitting diamond's into the air. Connected to the cloth, our hands still clasped, Grizzly and I shutter, and spasm.

[I miss you grandma.]

"Rude shelters, but argyle   (deceased)   +program." The radio hung in a tree house near the tree line utters, blasts of interference.

A four headed television hides beneath the rug, ready to spray out images, arcs round to the necklace pillow, melting butter, luminous crystal ball on the table, we hover our hands over lights, shivering hallows inside letters chiseled of ice weave, through our room. We watch a foam reflection – made strictly from

lamp shade on lamp shade, unfolded before Grizzly and I~

I take a break in a tan pillow case, follow a mirror maze out of our room, as she hovers over the glowing blue light, entranced.

[She was so beautiful.]

I wake up, a fragile, breakable exhale comes in through the windows.

Through a python repetition of half eyes, made clear by Grizzly, and her glowing crystal ball. She is snoring now. It smells like cigarettes, and I am itching my neck. The silk in my feeling has nested behind the itch. In the crystal ball, spinning anchors folded in the smoke, I walk the docks, it takes me in one way spatial relations, this hour. I finally get to Grizzly, and a low cloud pulls up sticks. I think there's been a reincarnation, because thought 432 comes to my mind:

432: A life can be a lovely beginning...

A small lewd, distracting light emerges. I rest the radio to her velvet thigh, as she snores. Rosemary grows arranged in its sound. Expressed as red language into our room, I massage her shoulders.

[It's gonna be okay, Grizzly.]

[She's in a better place now.]

RANDOM NATIONS

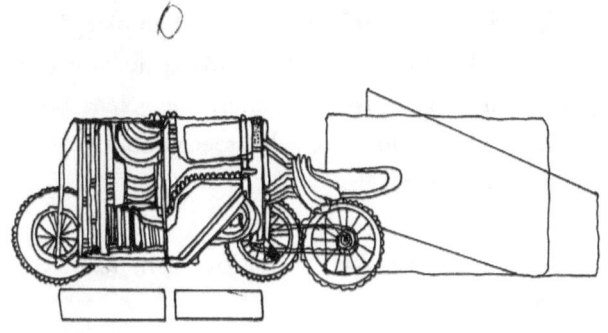

Our equilibrium strays, as we enter a fountain. Grizzly's pace is at an alligator's.

I chew Thorazine- and feel I hold hands with her like a ghost. Her heart hangs in the fountain -- For a moment I can see it being washed in the water.

The breaks on my body are in working order, so I can stumble around in the graveyards, searching for coyotes.

[You hear something?] Grizzly whispers. Her breath smells good, like fresh air.

We watch these wimpy dolls go whistling down into the fountains - and then the giraffes hang around, drinking up ties and strings from the department store- We sit down with a group of gypsies, and watch handlebar mustache guitars playing near the road. She hangs down her blue toenail polish toes over the cobbled street, and wiggles 'em.

We're in a motor car, going speeds of a light mare - going 250. We sleep in the

waves --Purple felt going by in the motor car window, and it's making Grizzly nervous. She says something like she had found settlements of accordion players while I was away, which I think is very interesting, and I start kissing her. The basic health is a system of tied together rowboats, we use in cooperation, by typing in signatures -a half-and-half foil mixture- lined equally, with copper, this is formed into a disk, and then placed within 'closets.'

Driving through old 1979 on the Nebraska highway, an old hoopty Cadillac Deville with slime and algae dripping down it like a paint job from the swamp thing. We bump along, silent, not speaking to each other. I smoke my cigarettes, she drives. The Delta blues plays on the radio. I make a few quick phone calls on our old yellow telephone.

"How many sewing machines can you sew at once?" Grizzly asks the subject on the other end, before putting on a latex mask over her head of a man's face, long shaggy hair. I sit passenger side, making paper plate hats, and sipping tea from Chinese cups as she drives and talks on the yellow dial tone, and then hands it back. I smell the boxes of 30 dozen eggs- as we pass a ghetto and watch a flying guitar pass over the town's water tower. We get to an arctic shell and park behind the structure. A metallic windmill turns behind the car, and I smoke cigarettes as she gets out dragging the long phone cord to the windmill.

Sealed, this base is foil we use from 1929 Christmas ornaments to glitch the computers of the system, our hoopty looks older than hell now, and rewire to our motherboard for an hour, Grizzly under the hood, and me under the brakes.

When Santa brings a package of old coins and a zombie, we pass around a fresh bottle of scotch, and with our new implement, subject retail stores to sell massages for under three dollars. At least it's what I think happened.

Cats wander the streets behind the newly hacked base, our outfits are a hand-sewn mess of collaged caterpillar webbings-

[This is our first experimental growing suits, using butterflies!] I tell Santa. I keep my eye on the zombie, he just stands there groaning, and staring at Grizzly's tits.

[I'm about to smack your little friend, Santa.]Grizzly says, holding up a shotgun, with the bottle in her other hand.

[Oh, he's harmless.] Santa says.

Back home, after our month-long road trip, (outside of the lab under the lake,) the idea we will train the butterflies from cocoon to land on our clothes, as a 'stage one' for the experiment is successful-

A lunch special comes in a box, it is the size of a teenager - we board the bus and get a lashing from our bus driver for our human-sized boxes of lunch--

I always eat my lunch in the first period.

Luscious Rum comes to my lips outside on the dock. From a string, I hook under the bus driver's seat - Grizzly and I are getting younger, and younger. She's eighteen, and I'm seventeen. I have been carrying ties and telephones in bikes and wagons all day in my box. I sell food I find at the food pantry to children-

141

younger than I, no matter what the expiration date.

I sell a kid a moldy sandwich, and he has to go to the school nurse.

Grizzly and I fly around in suit jackets, throwing warm, Hawaiian sweet rolls at the ceiling. The whole school starts a food fight - guitars enter rooms, hands, Open D, the band plays a NIN cover badly ~ Plastic containers, full of bread, are thrown at the teacher, camera's show cloth hands grabbing at loaves of bread-- eatable.

Alligators enter the cafeteria and begin eating some of the class.

Grizzly and I are fucking very hard in an armchair. At our feet, the television plays Dreamweaver, and I half-watch the music video while Grizzly bounces, half watching her breasts bobbing, moaning.

I see a kids spleen fall out of the alligator's enormous jaws. Grizzly and I keep fucking loudly overhead, swimming over the bloodbath. Exit and entrance are blocked up with dolls and teddy bears. Anyway, there's a long fat spirit now, lurching into the cafeteria, and it swipes at our armchair and bumps us. Grizzly pulls my cock out of her mouth, making a popping noise, and says duck. I do, and she grabs something off of a shelf nearby.

The chessboard flies into the fat spirit at top speed, I've never seen such a weapon, and gets caught inside something.

There is a groaning, choking sound, the alligator snaps at the arm and pulls the monster down into a more comfortable and sloppy eating position.

Grizzly gets back on my cock, easing it inside her vagina, slowly. She closes her eyes, and leans her head back, opening her mouth, exposing her teeth.

The radio plays: "Abraham, full of cookies, (rummage sale in his mind) flounder fish, eating pepper packets, spins the dice. Full of turtle shells changes bird feathers for sun and leaf costume. Foil helmet, and smells his hands, they do not want to smell like roast beef."

UP ME, FIX, YOU DID

We wake up in the afternoon, around noon. We are lounging in a giant wooden box full of Feathers. Grizzly turns and un-latches a motor, and strings tie candles over our heads, dangling on pulleys.

The bed lifts off of the ground floor, and we make our way to the rooftop. I sleep a little more, and Grizzly gets onto an eleva-tor from the love nest.

I turn over to glance a laboratory. Movements adjust me to a chiasm. We ride the depth my cues fold familiar 1965 of it all, in the stems of the feathers. I'm back in the Cadillac Deville, driving around Nashville, Tennessee. The radio plays Chinese music. I get my binoculars and attach them onto my head. I scan the perimeter. I'm staring into some field, adjusting the optic equipment. Grizzly makes some coffee in the passenger seat.

[Last night was fun.] She says.

She experiments on a tentacle between the machines. Grizzly makes fine adjustments, steady, while I drift highway and swal-low horizon, orchards unlocking in my closed eyes. The clock on our third night comes unfolding out of a table in the car. She wears a black dress, and sucks down oranges and then throws them at the feather bed, where our ostrich sleeps.

[Here!] She says, [Let's do it again.] Juice is secreted, pale, underwater.

I drift off.

[I'm having a lazy day.] I say.

Partway mirrors. I think I hear myself shout. The door floats ashore, lines the beach with fish and radios. We're back in the Cadillac in the desert.

Thin skeleton (keys) dangle in the rearview mirror. The radio's playing neon signal now.

[THIS JUST IN THE NEWS!] A voice breaks in.

[Two antelope and crab were seen climbing the tower of pizza!]

[A man in a bat mask was seen high-fiving Jesters today outside of a skyscraper, he had bleeding feet! The Jester and the man in the bat mask were cooking people in butterfly blood, one monster had big feet, ate butterflies, moths, he showed people there were faces on the wings before decapitating them.]

[Damn news.]Grizzly says, the percolator sound starting up.

[Coffees coming.]

[In other news, a swimming creature has been spotted in the lake, outside of Gettysburg.]

[it's us.] I say, looking over the cloud of smoke.

[Hmmm.] She continues.

[Two female rabbits were seen staring at each other today, at the park, sources said... While pink bears stood there in a mirror world!]

[Fuck you!] I shout, changing the dial to country.

PART | ONE

We're in the desert. I pick up a piece of ash, small, and stuffed

144

into the talons of a bird. We're outside of Nevada, near U.S. Route 50, or ninety, or… Grizzly is walking beside me, we're hand in hand in the open desert. Giant cactus hovers like people under the moonlight.

She leads me on (needle knitting the hours across the land, into one sad country.)

She smokes cigarettes, and I drink the last of our booze out of a flask, the liqueur has already woven in my breath. My rusted skeleton swims along the desert floor (feet lifted high above the ground, down along old abandoned mine shafts, and ancient river beds.)

Grizzly and I are like ghosts, crocheted, and hooked among swollen cactuses, mingled amidst the paper flowers emerging from the ground. Her and I wobble, floating along with a current, as if in a boat. Our arms are long, wooden oars. The sagebrush is our waters.

Grizzly and I warp, dangling across the atmosphere, in a changing, multiplying kind of a fleshly blur, like a sad country song suggests the sky be our new haven. We turn over the skin, see these solar raccoons with glass gear shifters, fumbling with the glass, using bones.

I'm a tube of oak, and I'm a wire connected tree. Grizzly forms soft tissue, melon eyes, gravel shoulders, grass vagina, and fertile hands. Glitter spills in and falls through us. The glass gear shifter torques, a loom weaves all of this together with precision. This is the hour of our shedding skin, in combination with the heavens… Grizzly plugs in the next lemon tile, which is white, and again we are floating in a coy pond ceiling, swimming in a paisley fabric for an hour or so.

The desert grows cold. It must be midnight.

Grizzly and I give each other small thigh tattoos as we wait in a cafe in the middle of Lush Rock, behind the cactus hotel. She orders three drinks back to back and gives me a tattoo with lights, and spells 'Idiots' among a part of my shoulder, and gets me laughing.

The bartender looks over at us curiously, hunched. The old man has a crook in his back, a disaster of some form of scoliosis.

She fills in the letters with another script: holy tomorrow, and I squint reading it.

We switch out the ink with neon yarn and she stitches a house into the wall of my neck. Cages cross beneath her shivering hand, as I stitch an old anchor on her wrist.

I sip the scotch, and the bartender just watches. No one else enters the hotel. Got the place to ourselves.

I'm sharpening wires, as she raises her legs over my head, and rests her thighs on my shoulders. I chill and sand glass in a slow mutation into a silver chest beneath my legs, and put the chest on over mine. Tunneling forward in the train of manatees, I glide through her, inside of mucus which winds a bucket of thread and stone into an ice field, where I perch upon a fence, studying my work.

Leaves weave up 'woven couch' before us, so we can lay back and warm-up, floating in Starfish. We ease back, flowing back and forth with the current of the desert.

Sipping water from a teal, bruised twilight, I lean back, drinking daisies from the glass temple of her babbling lips. She is restrained in a feeling of rusting, potassium rooms within her exhale, taking in just as much as aquamarine allows, sweeping now three of us, dimensional in her superNova. The neighbors bring us drinks and comment on sunset.

The bartender has shifted his weight into four or five new folks, and they hand us drinks from a waterfall.

[This is a nice place.] I say, winking down at an old lady. The little people perform plays in an oak chest beside us. Heat is pumped into the cafe. I draw up my plans for our next stretch of the drive, and Grizzly looks over the sheet, tells me I ain't

146

got no discipline of DNA strings. But I know different. It's a good plan.

With my fifth drink in my hand, I check in a cabinet and see if my pistol is in there.

[A spring-loaded now.] Grizzly speaks through her straw. I watch her lips.

[Yep. I say, holding up the gun.]

I see something out of the corner of my eye.

A little man, doing a jig. He dances around and around in tiny cowboy costume.

[Who's this?] I say to the bartender.

He just nods and looks away.

A third flinch from the bartender tells me something's out of order here. My perspective is like a layer of thin plastic which has been painted upon. So, Grizzly and I get up, walk over to the windows in the cafe, and water the windows with watering canteens, and by doing this, the flowers grow. The Nasturtiums, poppies, even the Orchids.

The bartender nods and pours us a few whiskeys.

After we drink them, we leave the cafe, and wander the desert, drifting around off of the ground, following these weird solvent lights around. We watch an orange fruit blinking at the horizon, the sunlight pouring into us like a glass of morning orange juice, from rising to pouring, floating to walking.

Inside of my hands, shelved along with the diaspora, sphere or ring finger of life perches a paper flower, Grizzly hugs one of those little people who has followed us here. She is in ecstasy, hugging the little cowboy person so tight.

We hit the cushions, in our pop up tent near the edge of Nevada, watching solar waves carve through the sky.

I feel my body as it falls downward, into a dark black vortex circa [1292] France. There are silverfish which have been painted onto the blank space before me.

Now, swimming circles through clouds under the seams, swimming in and out of spirals, trained like throwing knives, my body swims to the throwing wheel off in a great distance— I Scoop the air into a bucket, with the saltwater layers and cake layers, and am afraid of the possibility I might be drowning in cakes or some dormant isosceles which had been growing bigger and bigger out there, in the field.

My T-shirt tastes like breath, all scooped into a bucket, and I'm wearing Japanese 3d glasses, one red, and one blue. I sit upon a shelf in a medicine cabinet, I scoop up water, and throw it in my bucket, but from where?

Purple worms are an odd thing I've never seen until sleeping in the desert. The only way, it seems, to find them is by floating into the pond, like an inflatable dress with the geese, lounge in flotation for a while, and scan the surroundings. The micro world, in the crevices, designed around the dark, for the swim, or infinite equations housed in fear, into the bucket, shoveling great big algae smelling buckets of the swamp into your arms.

[Wouldn't it take up thirty floors of the cube?] I ask one of the geese calmly paddling past me in my polka dress. I hear electrocuted pauses, the static flows for a while, then erratically the static pops, coughing up signals, which scares away the goose.

Throughout the sounds in the swamp, there is so much dancing to be had, but I need to fill the bucket up with sludge and smells of algae, bird droppings, apple wings growing saturated behind me on a tree.

Machine houses park along the path, where oceans dissolve in, from the west. Fluids mix up their batter there, the baby batter.

The machine houses open up, loosen light, and cleaner air is enjoyed.

Science group #5 lands upon the ready-made star, behind us.

[How is everyone today?]

[Tired, but awake.]

A photographers technology, within a dead past, comes un-folded, from a briefcase. It unfolds, and a butterfly garden pops out of a clutched silver bottle in the doctor's lab coat.

Sweating, the doctor hurries all of the scientists along, into a train station, they board the train, and I watch them ride up over the mountains.

Unknowingly clutched at its

disappearing edges, Grizzly handles a

fine, trimmed razor, aiming it at specimens.

[Shall I?] She asks, as stars let open the secret doors in the wall, followed by a million light lurks, pretending to be white snow

beneath our carpet, in the desert.

I wake with a lantern, it's probably five or six am, because I can see the horizon, and the sun is coming up, and it is cold.

A gathering of dimensions tatters down, into newsprint faces

through the entryway, by Numbered hours on the shore.

Grizzly and I are drafting a 'boat' in secret

designed

eyes.

Both in a need to kiss.

Tortures make

sense taped later into braille.

Groups five and six, transplanted

with guitar strings,

water, crowns, cardboard,

heads, a chair, the tabletop,

dust covers, papers, yellow, data,

strings, edge, sky, coffee, sit, cigarette, folded, motionless, cactus, car, shoulders, neat, warm.

We sit, broadcasting on the station at midnight, from a makeshift rooftop we built out of 'found' plywood.

Piles of transmission hang around in 'Michelle's' flowers,
which we've been keeping track of for the last hour.

Going within the silk hair of the universe, so to speak, we're
dancing right through these radio transmissions

       from Russian

       satellite-like butter on a flame.

The night is shadowed

In language,

ghostly faces of 'Michelle,' the secrets she whispers to

Vladimir at the dark patches

of the house.

Little men face us

behind the laundry room door – little men in trouble.

Lawn gnomes hand-painted and set up in the laundry room, it
looks cool, all of the colors. The Russian's speak

Languages I've never heard now,

  corroded in the living room.

I strap down a pair of binoculars to inspect their grid, par-
ticularly in

the kitchen,

and watch noodles climbing wallpaper to spell names.

[Hmm. Grizzly, take a look at these names, do those mean

anything to you?]

She straps on the goggles.

Takes a squinting look.

[A Soviet gardener, I've heard
of him, yes. Write this down.]

She spells out his name for me and I write it in the logbook.

She hands me back the goggles, and I watch other strange
fruit, wiggle woggle, toggle in the

Static,

A late-night pill forms in the static,

I watch my hands through the Static,

silk hair is made of

entangled static with

noodles, cooked to perfection.

Walls corrode soft,

warm.

Letters, inside of an

orange peel, I find

the sky full of them.

Retro-fitted clouds are perched in a porch deck.

Circular, we find enough time to

escape Tuesday. Grizzly and I board our ship and hover low
over the fluffy sage.

Onboard, in ivy shelves,

the rooms pool into a cup.

Science group # 1 decides to arouse the sphere, and call in-
dentations a brain, and wearing spectacles

Grizzly is naked,   laced in the diamond
shadows.

All the groups put iris around the doorways of the cafe, the
makeshift station, and our Cadillac.

With a divine cut in the stone "biology," saw-blades dissolve
behind me, [They are looking for something.] I say to Grizzly.

Latticework crosses morning before I wake. Another night

passed so quickly, I must be aging faster now, our garden pours
into the cup.

                    Woven lime golden screws,
   little portraits
   of strawberry, our kitchen appears. Grizzly stands in her underwear and makes us some coffee.
   Picture pours cups of coffee,
   Cherry lines, ligaments,
   cortex, an opening appears.
                    [The lab's going out today, we should check
on the previous rooms, collide our data somehow, what do you
think, hon?]
   Making one tall, winding building, I say:
   [I'm in! Just need coffee.]
   The radio spirals back into last night
                    strung together through the
   chimney to a person,
   To a diamond to the scissors, rinsing out the present moment, doing backflips, cutting pictures, sewing curtains, ripping
clothing, gnawing waffles, dripping syrup, listing panels, wooden
samples,
   a Good old radio, farming pharmacy.
   When the electrostatic was
   left on, radio washes the windows
   with small, shallow pools
   Surges up radon, it can disconnect molecules of
    iron, let alone bones and flesh, then we have a choice, the
alley, where,
   around the corner
   disturbed birds disappear upon a wire, or
   Lost, we will wake up
   in cages and hours–
   And forget about all this for me, I'm going to the alley.
   The waves of light, course

upward, breath strokes,

headaches,   finally

     a number.

Caving in, the old hat seeds

locked by key, because of Grizzly and I,

rooms in a golden

entry, digits and an

armchair maze,

 Wooden panels

  form into the sea.

      A citadel rises from the desert floor and a chop- Chop,

chopping sound,

  Some part of a jumpsuit laying lonely in casing, jagged edges

of

  the Radio wave, sending nutrients to a

  house full of

  removed dust. A caused

   black mold

  from the circuit board of tulip danglings',

   just enough light

  for twigs, invoices,

  built of treasure chest houses, stairs,

  shooting stars,

  fish in brass,

  escaping.

The Steeple rises out of clouds,

 scaring the sky into our one

 room with numbers, (sawdust,

Dream, fishes.)

Grizzly Plants

 splattered paint beneath our

separate rooms breathe,

  nesting her hands in the clock,

  and a Chandelier, to catch back up with her distorted body.

I say [Sweet,] I help her pressure chain the Chandelier, and we both catch back up in the cafe.

The bartender cleans out glasses.

The little people are leaping, in leisure, morphed all around the bar. We watch from the window as giant legs cross in the sky.

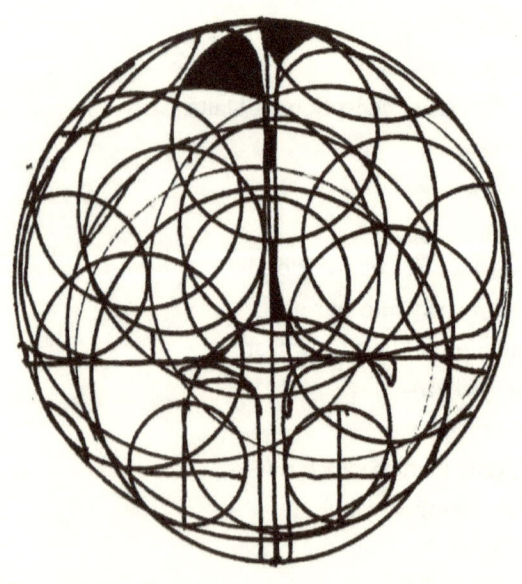

I am full of air cells growing into parts of my skeleton, my teeth have all fallen to the wood floor. In, through the slats, a scary recognition; I am wearing a pair of my jealous/luscious titanium skull/ from this state of mind, I can purchase a ticket to a surveillance film, to get my mind lapping on the track it used to. My clothes are made of moss, lichen, snails, and I hang along the Veranda, making perfect puzzles from the screen and chairs and tables... A theater. Hmm.

She watches from a front pew in the theater, Motorcycle-paste-to-paper, her body lifting to the roof from within her chair before the screen. She climbs light, the audience mystified by her levitation. After a time she makes her way back, down ropes, built out of hair and thread, and clothing, and socks. On-screen, a man pulls out a bag of stone, with a television dragging behind him. All sounds are made from paper bags, who are playing somewhere in a room on the third floor.

A video of snakes nesting plays in the theater. Others, now float up from their seats and sing songs as I sob in my seat, watching this all. I sip my tonic through the unreasonable tears, shaking the liquid back down my throat, and witness their hair made of ropes, lifting them from their seats into the rafters. I begin lactating nests of birds, clumped up, deranged red admirals, falling out of my breasts.

I release a diamondback snake from my top hat, and the snake slithers down along my stomach, and into the seats, and disappears. A thing like this only happens when I'm drinking.

I extend my hand, except the formula, sip my Vodka down down down.

I am witness to drip-pressed-stomach-modules I've never seen, pumping on screen. Fish enter the air of the musty theater, little pink ones, little swimming-Pink-fighting-goldfish in the-black-water. One goes down my pants leg, and slips around my sex with its mouth, sucking slowly, and then randomly nibbling my pubic hair. In a way, we came here, because we were aroused by fish sex.

The silhouettes of strung together puppets dance in the back, near a curtain.

[Madison is the first puppets name,] Grizzly says, grasping hold of my hand. Her face is as I remembered it, soft, white. Her hair is jet black, combed, and tightly strung into braids.

[Oh, thank God, it's you. I couldn't take it…]

[Shhh.] She says.

I slug back a long pull of Vodka, and she slaps the bottle to the ground.

[You shouldn't be drinking!]

[I know!] I sob, grappling for the bottle under my seat, and clutching it, I hide it away for later.

Grizzly next to me, her hair is connected to the rafters, pulling the skin of her face up in a monstrous way.

Kaleidoscope: We are in Milwaukee. We fly into Chicago on our fish genitals, the tiny horseshoe puppets behind us.

[Were going ninety-four miles per hour,] she says, kissing me, and drooling in ecstasy. [Make sure to secure your goggles, ah-hhh. Ohhh.]

We fly through Cleveland, then Erie. My cheeks flap at eighty-six miles per hour. We fly over Randolph, a curve is taken around back, the puppet lets down its bodily ladder and Grizzly and I the ship away through further loops, the land down at a wax museum of some kind. My goggles fog up, and I hear the sound of a Turkey to my right. I hear the sound of a steady crank lifting a bridge. I defog the goggles, and we share a smoke at the entry of the bridge. [Where are we?] She says.

[I think we went back into the past, there is a castle.] I say. A wax museum hovers in the fog.

[it's a wax museum, Honey. Not a Castle.]

[Oh, yeah right.] Hand pulleys and cranks are lifted by an old

Finnish dude - who smiles and shows one tooth - laughing at us maniacally. We stand and smoke, ignoring the man.

The shoulders of Grizzly hang low, to the leaves, as she picks up a pile of scattered papers. I hold her by her elbow, and we open a birdcage together. A baby pterodactyl squeaks inside.

She places her fingers across mine, and we grasp an old key next to the pterodactyl, and we turn it together, into the lock.

Here come the swans and ghosts, the closet door spinning its wheels, and us watching ourselves spun through a dark room.

Kaleidoscope:

Lights flashing red above, we reach the mechanics room, through a long lit tunnel behind the birdcage. Hand turns on a crank and long ropes in this darkness, the "Robert" spins in a chair and faces the two of us.

[Yes, how may I help you?]

[Door, Jackass! It's us. Open the door!] Grizzly shouts. His eyes are painted in with black paint on wooden marbles, his skin and his jacket are the same awful glowing green beneath the oppressive black tunnel.

The "Robert" programs in a set of digits on his grimy keypad, and unlocks the door. Behind is a secret lake in the walls of our house ~ where the swans go to. The door closes, and the "Robert" disappears.

Grizzly is horny, she undresses, and folds her hands over her head, curling her toes and thighs together, and bending over in a swan dive --

I jump in after her and we wander ink, to a place buried beneath the lake. I follow through the dark water, looking for the bottoms of her feet, and small of her back. I taste algae and know we are home.

When we get underground, a familiar orange taste is found in the furniture. We shake off the water in the base, and Grizzly opens up the broken-down house walls on a hillside on her own, knowing well her strength; only at dawn is this entrance available. We meet here beneath the lake, now, every winter, year after year.

I drag my fingers across the sample shelf, focus my bones in the metal. She whispers: [Sorry, Meadow] This opens another sublevel door, and we board with cases, rotating on levers, and pick our seats in the back of the ship.

The Tower of Pizza

Our ship swings out on thin, brown packaging string, over the lake below -- forward -- (adjusts mechanics,) its walls groaning and reversing. Moss spiders wheel away in the underwater sounds of bubbling, rumbling, as we exit the base, and the ship dislodges from its post, into the night.

Back on the second level, we finally drift to sleep. I focus on her breath; It's soft golden yarn, and her thin, warm arms curled up beside me, forming a pocket of heat. The boat oozes flowers as we move along, puttering: Petunias, and Roses, and Orchid flowers, and Nasturtiums, and Poppies, and Lavenders. In her eyes and mouth, and nostrils I get pleasantly lost, searching out with finger, and map. Dripped, in pumpkin, the saliva of the dogs (...) Me, I'm lost in still frames. I watch Grizzly turn and reflect doorknob pinstripe off the golden doorknob for effect, then we go neon, and I'm underwater, in my neon sub-suit, combing the floor of the lake for treasure. Grizzly is behind me, her glowing neon sub-suit is orange and mine is pink. We comb along the floor, slowly move through the deep blue dark, in the peaceful warm soup of the neon sub-suits.

I smell creosote, and gas from the suit storage in the garage. I pull up a small shell and inspect it. The numbers are written there and appear for a moment. I log them in my memory, and then I watch as the numbers fall off of the side of the shell and into the water, where they float off in the current. This is a sequel to our show from two Sundays ago: except in our episode centaurs were floating around in the garden above us, and I was inspecting closer with a magnifying glass to see if I could locate the treasure, and those centaur shaped balloons floated above us, and whatnot.

I open a hatch underground, and watch the snails on the lake bottom, cling for dear life to the edge. I walk through a small changing room, with another pressurized door, and change out of the sub-suit, watching the pink light span the enclosure. After me, the neon of Grizzly's suit enters the hatch and closes the floor. We are processed, and spit out through a hole, into bed in our new clothes. A clown with fluffy garters, and a fisherman with a Donkey named Egor for a head walk up to the bed.

Slowly Slowly, we begin to realize our bed is in the middle of an open football field. This place is peopled with children who are playing basketball. I shout:

[Saw Blade Season, little tikes! We're gonna get you all nice, big saw blades this year, and a Tower of Pizza! We're gonna find it!] I'm in my nightgown, yelling this gibberish through a white megaphone, my voice Squawk's from interference. Now, in the corner of my eye, I can see a man is hunched down beneath the bed installing leather painted doors under there.

A kid runs up, and he's carrying a basketball or it's a Pizza?

[Top down at the Tower of Pizza.] I shout into the foggy field, over the megaphone. He runs away, screaming, and crying, and a girl hands me a peppermint. I eat it through the Egor helmet and watch sunlight enter into our bedroom on the ship. I taste the mint freshness, and close my eyes, see moonlight, crossing over the field. I get on my knees and fondle Grizzly's breasts, a moonstone she had placed on her bosom reflects in the twilight.

Horses ride through the field behind her and I. The children who were playing Basketball run with their balls over their heads, into the ocean. The ocean engulfs them in big black waves. We reach midnight.

I open a hatch in the side of Grizzly's stomach and see the squid rummaging through boxes inside her. It inks the water and hides there in the blue glow.

~ A distant morning ship crosses above us, we wake, and watch it pass, and hold each other's hands- A keyring of skeletons takes off, into the water, floats, and lifts away the snakeskin handle, and folds up in terra cloth, behind the ship, pulling on us, back into the dreams.

[What is this?]Grizzly whispers from beyond.

[It's winter when I see my hands from a chandelier.] I say.

[Fly traps are hanging somewhere - they disappear, paper birds flying around-]We sink together, deeper down, our hands clenched full of roses and bouquets of gypsy flowers, and Orchids, and Lavender, Poppy, Petunias, and Calendula. Wrapping around our wrists, Nasturtiums are growing along the bone, these flowers I give her.

The Layer of pterodactyl claw

In the morning we stand naked together in our shower. I watch shampoo lift out all of these versions of a dark inky octopus from Grizzly's hair, through the fog. (Thirty-five balloons rise from somewhere in Grizzly's hair) out of the room, and into the suction fan above, where they pop. POP! POP! POP! POP! Outside, I watch the lawn as apples roll around in circles. Fish float away in the steam, as I wash her belly, steadying myself against the tile wall. Light curls from her fins, reflecting multiple colors against the shower walls.

It's dawn, we hold hands, board the shuttle with lawn gnomes, and cross the pond. The lawn gnomes stare at us, they wear apple shoes on their little feet.

Walking with candy cane crutches, the shampoo smell shadows behind Grizzly. The lawn gnomes help lift the helium balloons out of Grizzly and walk them out to the door of the shuttle where they are released as they are every day. From a first look, strawberry paintings land, exploding red nectar, into the streets. In the street lamps, fuzing to light, all filtered and half flickering are broken flashes to illuminate this strawberry explosion, cause bears gonna be painted on the roads, now. Long, loopy shadows which the little men start to bring into focus beneath a large pterodactyl-like bird with machine gears on its moving parts bring this machine into the hull of the ship, using a leash, the thing squawking and ripping at the alloy doors.

[Good girl, Isabelle.] Grizzly says, petting her alloy feathers. The pterodactyl tastes some water from the lake. Grizzly and I wash white latex rubber off of our sex~ Two young boys sit on a couch ashore, drinking beers below. The shuttle arrives at [space station 109] on time, as usual. Now, I help carry harps to a play, wooden room.~ The harps generate string nests, for our new machine bird, Izabelle, as well as new doorways, doors where we all enter, the little men, and pterodactyl, and Grizzly and I put on our white space suits in a glass chamber, above the lake. I watch fish below, curving along the green lake water, eating algae. Grizzly and I, our pterodactyl, and our lawn gnome hologram eat leaves together ~

Harps fly over the changing room in the ship. Ladders come down from the glass station above. We exit, line the shore outside, watching beaver and frogs.

[Beaver cleaver!] I say, smoking a cigarette. The suit sucks outgas from our Mercedes Benz tanks, and Grizzly chuckles. We hang over the Columbia plateau, near an old paper factory, sipping wine. A local wing nut sits nearby drinking beer, with his friend, and throwing the cans at passing freight trains: "Apollo" Grizzly mutters, and I nod in agreement, dialing a phone number on the arm of my suit jacket, inhaling the smoke.

xxx-xxx-xxxx

Phone number redacted for privacy. -ZH

The story of the pterodactyl and the pig

They turned a lake into a television show outside of a small town in Georgia, on the 5th of May. Photographers came on over to the lake, sitting on the shore, trying desperately to focus their Nikon and Canon lenses ~

A half bird woman came along and wiped out all of the photographer's with little force. Me, and my partner just set up a couch, and an ice chest. We just sit, watching the television as the bird destroys any intruders with fell swoops of doom. People try boating on our TV, and skiing with the family, etc but to no avail. Our nasty bird is a monster. It consumes full boats with jaws the size of a house. It swallows whole cars, and George swigs his beer.

"D'jaw see that one, that was a 55 chevy, Tommy!"

"Yep," I say. "I have seen it! That bird's a monster, she hates intruders, sure does like us around, ain't it, George?"

"Gee," George shouts. "I suppose she does, Tommy." Gulp.

"Well, keep cars coming! She's a hungry bastard!" I shout.

"I wanna real show, you know, right here!" I say.

"They'll come, don't you worry Tommy. More cars will come." We sip beer and watch the lake on our TV. I finish my beer, crack another.

"Ahhh, Life is good."

"Sure is." The police arrive, and Sargeant Bill Signy, (the fucker) he points a black pistol at us on our couch, says freeze.

Tells us were trespassin'. He's gonna brain us right here on this swag couch.

I hold up my fresh beer, and pour it into my mouth, while, lumbering sixteen feet tall behind bitch cop is our nerdy birdy, love of our life, eats right arm with pistol first, (elegantly) I might add. Snacks softly on the screaming torso of what used to be officer Signy. Then, like lettuce, the legs, leaves those nasty feet in place by the car. Guess she doesn't like that part. Eats the car, leaves the tires.

So, tires and feet... Could be bad for us, George and I stagger (drunk now) from the couch to the crime scene, blood everywhere.

"Good birdie." George pets the mechanical plating of the bird's wings, and she squawks.

"Now for these." George kicks the tires, and the shoes away to an outhouse near the parking lot and leaves it all there.

"A midnight snack," I say.

"Yeah," George says. We make a sign which reads NEED BEER, and set it up next to us on the couch, while we polish off the thirty racks in our ice chest ~

Laughing.

****

SWEEPing in the FIELD, Grizzly talks on her CELLPHONE, and I clean my FEET before we enter our TOWER.

We are wearing these heavy tourmaline bodysuits, the heavy rock is insulated and hard to move inside, but we mosey through the crash fields, both connected to unraveled string from the pockets of 'space-Drift' in the distance. A slow, collapsing radio station broadcasts as we stumble through tornadoes coiled heavily on the surface.

Bindweed holds our feet, and then rips away, as we trudge through the mess of collisions. Her wing follows after my wing, and we communicate over radio, searching sleek hair, all those dangling, long, galaxies of cheap wigs, hung on church walls, so to speak...

Little forts gather in a place, tangled up in branches, and bindweed. We follow spruce trees circular, up along the castle walls, mutations unfolding,

orange juice comes to her lips, cranberry sauce to mine, bread, tomatoes, lettuce, french fries, beer, cigarettes, gravy, sponges, dish soap, trash bags.

Grizzly talks on her phone as she washes in the sponges and dish soap. A turtle passes, name Albert.

[Hi, Albert!] I say. He stops and looks up, cannot see me, and pauses there, looking around.

I dress in trash bags and drink beer, eat some french fries. Albert, unsure, passes us slowly up the steps of the castle.

[I call him little-battle.] Grizzly says, rinsing the water off of her nipples, and drying her legs with a towel, before re-suiting.

We get to the top chamber of the tower and she starts taking my plastic bag off and throws away my beer. I watch ivy grow along with the window, sagging down.

[You shouldn't be drinking.] She says and smiles at the corners of her lips.

Grizzly is bending time/space with her wings. The wind is blowing in the fields below, sending sharp, high-pitched songs through its levers.

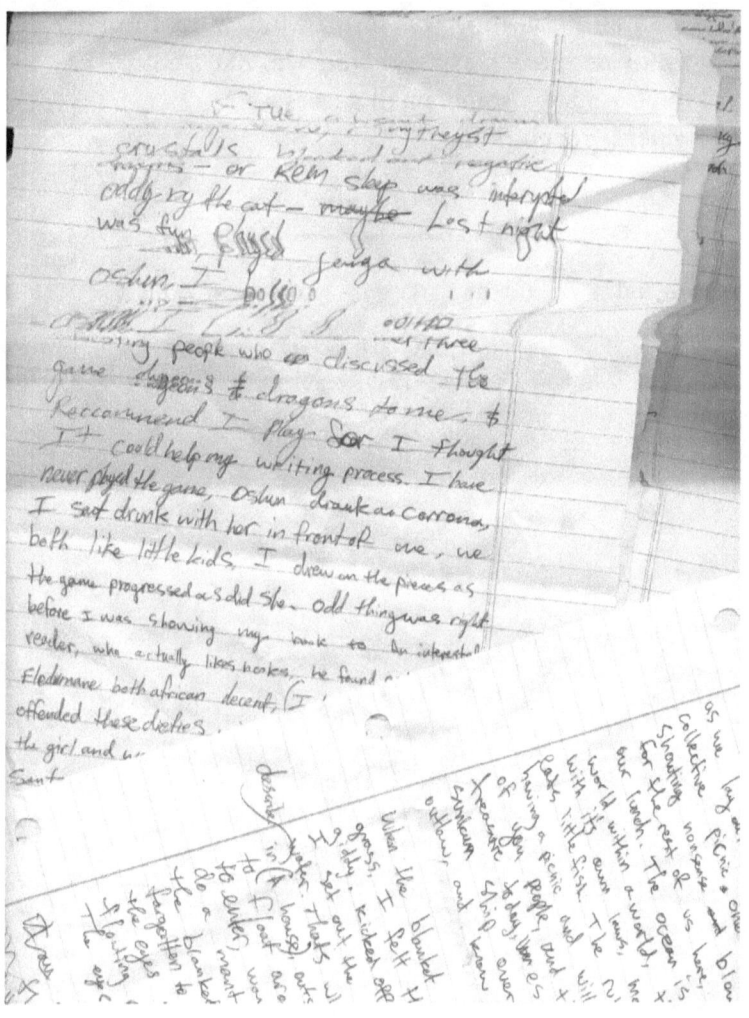

Fin Sorrel rides a bicycle, and loves animals.

Pski's Porch Publishing was formed July 2012, to make books for people who like people who like books. We hope we have some small successes. **www.pskisporch.com.**

323 East Avenue
Lockport, NY 14094
www.pskisporch.com